THE JOURNEY OUT

A GUIDE FOR AND ABOUT LESBIAN,

GAY, AND BISEXUAL TEENS

THE JOURNEY OUT

A GUIDE FOR AND ABOUT LESBIAN, GAY, AND BISEXUAL TEENS

BY RACHEL POLLACK AND
CHERYL SCHWARTZ

VIKING

VIKING
Published by the Penguin Group
Penguin Books USA Inc., 375 Hudson Street, New York, New York 10014, U.S.A.
Penguin Books Ltd, 27 Wrights Lane, London W8 5TZ, England
Penguin Books Australia Ltd, Ringwood, Victoria, Australia
Penguin Books Canada Ltd, 10 Alcorn Avenue, Toronto, Ontario, Canada M4V 3B2
Penguin Books (N.Z.) Ltd, 182-190 Wairau Road, Auckland 10, New Zealand

Penguin Books Ltd, Registered Offices: Harmondsworth, Middlesex, England

First published in 1995 by Viking, a division of Penguin Books USA Inc.
Published simultaneously in Puffin Books

1   3   5   7   9   10   8   6   4   2

LIBRARY OF CONGRESS CATALOGING-IN-PUBLICATION DATA
Pollack, Rachel.
The journey out : a book for and about gay, lesbian, and bisexual teens /
Rachel Pollack, Cheryl Schwartz.   p.   cm.
Includes bibliographical references and index.
Summary : Suggests how gay, lesbian, and bisexual teenagers may discover their
sexual orientation, find self-acceptance, come out, cope with prejudice,
and deal with religious and political issues.
ISBN 0-670-85845-5. — ISBN 0-14-037254-7 (pbk.)
1. Gay teenagers—United States—Juvenile Literature. 2. Lesbian teenagers—
United States—Juvenile Literature. 3. Bisexuals—United States—Juvenile Literature.
4. Coming out (Sexual orientation)—United States—Juvenile Literature. [1. Homosexuality.]
I. Schwartz, Cheryl. II. Title.
HQ76.3.U5P655 1995 305.23'5—dc20   95-14276   CIP   AC

Printed in USA
Set in Sabon

THIS BOOK IS DEDICATED, IN LOVING MEMORY, TO EDWARD HYMOFF, WHO INSPIRES MY LIFE AND WORK.

—R. P.

TO THE YOUNG PEOPLE I'VE WORKED WITH—YOU'VE CHANGED MY LIFE FOREVER.

—C. S.

CONTENTS

ACKNOWLEDGMENTS

Writing this book has been a journey for both of us, one which parallels the journey toward understanding and acceptance upon which you are embarking.

We were strangers who came together because we shared a common purpose: our wish to help you come to terms with your sexual orientation, to learn about yourself, to understand and accept yourself. While we were learning about you from talking to you, working with you, and seeing you through your trials and tribulations, we also learned about each other.

Cheryl says: This book is the culmination of my own experiences as an "out" teenager in suburban America and as an adult who has worked with lesbian, gay, bisexual, and transgendered youth for the past eight years. The most wonderful aspect of writing this book has been working with Rachel, a nice Jewish heterosexual "granny" whom I have come to trust completely. Growing up lesbian in the most accepting family possible and working in the gay community have kept me shielded from much of the heterosexual world. I thank Rachel for her openness, acceptance, and willingness to learn about me and about us.

Rachel says: First I want to say how much I like and admire the young people who have chosen to be interviewed for this book. Although they come from very different backgrounds and have been affected by the discovery of their sexual orientations in different ways and at different times in their lives, they have all displayed the courage to speak freely about the dangers and rewards of being who they are. Many of Cheryl's own experiences mirror the stories of these young people. At the heart of her work with them are her courage and honesty—strengths which gave us both the inspiration to write this book.

It is our fervent wish, and that of the young people who contributed to this book, that our readers who are coming to terms with their sexuality will discover that they are not alone, that there are many dedicated people like Cheryl who will reach out to them.

It is also our wish that parents and other adults who read this book will find new ways to understand and alleviate some of the rejection and isolation the young people they know and care for may be feeling.

We would like to thank the young people who opened their lives to us. For their enthusiastic participation in the photo shoot for the book cover, special thanks go to Jason Newland, Andie Montoya, Alvin J. Fung, Karen Susnitzky, Emily Clair, Desiree L. Waters, David B. Moschel, and Prudence Browne, members of YES (Youth Enrichment Services), a lesbian, gay, bisexual, and transgendered youth group of New York City's Lesbian and Gay Community Services Center.

We offer special thanks to the following organizations and people: The Gay, Lesbian and Bisexual Community Services Center of Colorado, Inc.; The Bridges Project; The Hetrick-Martin Institute; The Sexual Minority Youth Assistance League (SMYAL); Time-Out Youth; Lavender Youth Recreation and Information Center (LYRIC); The Healthy Boston Coalition for Lesbian, Gay, Bisexual, and Transgendered Youth; Lambda Legal Defense and Educational Fund, Inc.; The National Advocacy Coalition on Youth and Sexual Orientation; Parents, Families and Friends of Lesbians and Gays (PFLAG). Our deep gratitude to Mary Fairbanks, M.D., Bentley Smith, M.D., Reverend Elder Dr. Charley Arehart, Frances Kunreuther, Jenie Hall, Rea Carey, Barbara Bickart, Bridget Hughes, Carol Gush, Rabbi Susan Freeman, Rabbi Steven Foster, Rabbi Daniel Goldberger, Joyce Freeman,

Ph.D., Patrick Agan, Howard Selinger, Ph.D., Erika Lindholm, Al Silverman, and Melanie Cecka. We also want to thank our friends and families who trusted and believed in our vision.

Most of all, we would like to thank Stephanie Hutter, our editor, who believed in this book every step of the way and made it possible.

CHAPTER ONE

WHO AM I?

"I was offended when people called me gay in the third and fourth grade. In middle school they called me a lesbian and I denied it. On my way to gym class I would shut my eyes so I wouldn't have to see anyone. When I was sixteen I didn't want to believe what I was. But now it's my turn to be happy about who I am." —Lynn, 19

"I knew about myself in junior high school. I didn't think I was wrong or evil, but I thought that no one else in Wyoming was gay." —Brandon, 19

"I had difficulties, but not because I didn't accept myself. My difficulties came when I got tired of lying to others." —Will, 17

It may have started early. At five you felt you were somehow different from your friends. It wasn't anything you could put a name to, just an indescribable sensation in the pit of your stomach.

When you were nine, someone called you a "fag" when you tripped over third base on your way to home plate. Or at ten you were called a "lezzie" when you shimmied up the rope faster than anyone else in the fifth grade. You started having migraine headaches or stomachaches from the uncertainty that hung like a cloud over your head. Why, you wondered, do the kids call me names? What do these words mean? Do they know something about me that I don't?

Or perhaps it started in junior high. Now you know the meaning of the funny feeling in the pit of your stomach that hits every time you are with your math teacher. You have a crush, and it sends you to the math lab every day after school for the extra attention. You make yourself a promise that you are going to love math forever. You hang on your teacher's every word—and you get very good at math. For the first time in your life, you have feelings for someone of the same sex, and it's exciting but kind of scary. And even now you may not have a name for it. But after a period of time you realize that your teacher is only interested in seeing you do well in math, not in returning your affection.

Or maybe you are now in high school. You've over-

2

heard your parents wondering late at night why you haven't started dating. You smile to yourself remembering the intimate conversation you had with your best friend as you came out to each other just last week, when you finally put a name to your feelings. You have a new understanding of your sexual orientation. And knowing that you are not alone helps. You've just taken your first steps along the road of self-discovery and self-acceptance.

Now the real questions begin.

WHAT IS SEXUAL ORIENTATION?

Sexual orientation is defined by which gender (or genders) you have feelings of attraction and affection toward. These feelings can be expressed in a variety of ways, emotionally and physically. Heterosexuality, or "being straight," is having feelings of affection for and being attracted to people of the opposite gender. Homosexuality, from the Greek *homo* (same) and the Latin *sexus* (sex), is having those feelings for people of the same gender as yourself. "Lesbian" refers to a homosexual woman and "gay male" is the term for a homosexual man. "Gay" can also be used as a general term including male and female homosexuals and bisexuals, as we will use it on occasion in this book. Bisexuality means feeling attraction and affection towards both men and women.

We are all sexual beings. Current research strongly

3

suggests that our sexual orientation is determined from birth, as part of our genetic inheritance. *The realization of our sexual orientation can happen at any time in our lives.*

WHAT IF I'M NOT SURE WHAT MY SEXUAL ORIENTATION IS?

Affectionate and sexual feelings can be very confusing. One day you may be sure of your sexual orientation, the next day equally sure you were wrong. Some of this confusion may come from inside. Self-knowledge is an ongoing process—you can't expect an "orientation lightbulb" to suddenly appear over your head. You've already received many messages about who you should be from family and friends, from church and society. You could be torn between living up to others' expectations of you and being true to your own feelings. A lot of things can stand in the way of coming to terms with your sexual orientation. But there are ways to sort out the confusion.

If you're hanging out with or dating friends of the opposite gender to find out who you are, or just to please your parents or to keep peers from harassing you, it's okay. If you feel you're ready to start dating same gender friends, that's okay too. Experimentation is natural and can reveal a lot about who you are—as long as you look out for your own safety and live up to your own expectations, not someone else's.

You may want to read books about lesbians, gays, and bisexuals. They not only provide you with the information you need to work out your feelings, they are proof that you are not alone in your questions. You can also share your feelings and thoughts with people you trust, people who care about you, and gain support from them: family members, friends, counselors, doctors, teachers, those involved in a gay community center. You don't have to go it alone. Lots of people can help you maintain your physical and emotional well-being—and taking good care of yourself is the best thing you can do during this sometimes difficult (but not impossible) time in your life.

You may find that you are not lesbian, gay, or bisexual after all but just exploring your sexuality. That's okay too—it's healthy to think about sexuality. Exploration doesn't determine your sexual orientation, it simply helps you discover your own true feelings. *No one can ever talk you into being someone you're not.*

DO I HAVE TO HAVE SEX TO KNOW IF I'M GAY?

No! Having sex before you're emotionally and intellectually ready for it is more likely to create confusion than to resolve it. Being lesbian, gay, or bisexual is about more than having sex. It's about attraction, affection, how you see yourself and your place in society. Some young people have discovered ways to be intimate with their partners without having sex. Talking, spending time together, hugging, kissing, massaging, and holding hands are all ways to share affection for someone you care about. Some people choose to meet their own sexual needs through masturbation. Many young people today choose not to have sex at all. For those who feel it is the right time to become sexually active, there are many responsible ways to protect yourself and your partner from sexually transmitted diseases, HIV/AIDS, and pregnancy. You'll read about this frequently in this book. *It is essential to be safe in everything you do.*

WHAT IF I DON'T LIKE BEING GAY?

Discovering your awakening sexual feelings isn't particularly easy for anyone, gay or straight. And it certainly isn't easy being gay in a straight and frequently homophobic society. You may be feeling confused, isolated, and misunderstood. You may feel guilty or even angry with yourself. Jeremy, age 15, remembers asking, "'Why did I make such a stupid choice?' I blamed myself for not being straight like everyone else I know." Please note that homosexuality isn't a "choice," just as heterosexuality isn't a "choice." We become aware of our affectionate feelings and attraction toward others as we grow up, regardless of what those feelings are. It's as simple and straightforward as that. The choice is whether or not you are going to accept yourself.

Ann, 16, also had problems accepting her sexuality. She says:

In the beginning I just wanted to escape all of the anger, guilt, frustration, and the hurt that I felt. I really believed that I was letting everyone down, including myself, when I realized that I was a lesbian. To escape, I started drinking a lot and doing drugs. I even took too many pills once, hoping my bad feelings would all go away. My grades fell, and I tried to quit the soccer team. Luckily, my parents and my coach wouldn't let me do that. Soccer saved my life. Somehow, I found the courage to ask my parents if I could see a psychologist. They thought this was a good idea because they wanted me to be cured. I liked talking to my therapist; he was very helpful. With his help I cured my self-hatred and started on the road to accepting my sexuality.

When you are hurting, there are many things you can do that don't put you in danger. Do something you enjoy, such as writing in a journal, doing exercise or yoga, or pursuing a hobby. Get involved—find an activity, sport, or cause you'd like to join. Sing, play music, or just talk with friends. Do whatever makes you feel good about yourself.

If you are depressed or feeling desperate, talk to someone immediately. *You do not have to talk about your sexual orientation with that person.* You only have to tell her or him that you are feeling bad and that you need help. After you get the help you need and after you feel comfortable, you can decide whether or not to talk about your sexuality.

Above all else, be curious about what life has to offer and what you have to give, without messing up your mind or body. Be curious enough to find out how you will work things out. Get help when you need it. Don't give up. *And always remember: you are not alone!*

DO I HAVE TO BE "OUT" TO BE GAY?

No! Telling other people about your sexual orientation—"coming out"—is a personal decision. Whether or not you are ready to come out depends on how strong you feel, what questions you are willing and able to answer, how much support you need and can expect from those who care about you, and your stage of self-acceptance. You also need to consider the nature of your relationships with your family, friends, and community. In the beginning it is important to tell only the people you trust the most, people who won't tell others and who won't hurt you. Chapter 3 will help you decide whom to tell, and when and how to tell them. *It is always easier to come out when you feel a sense of self-acceptance and your self-esteem is high.*

DO I HAVE TO FIT A STEREOTYPE?

No! In fact there are no stereotypical ways to be lesbian, gay, or bisexual. You will, however, find that a lot of people have stereotypical views of what gays and lesbians look and act like—that they all act, dress, and move the same way. Some of the stereotyping comes from ignorance, misinformation, or an oversimplified view of the world. Too frequently these views are the creation of homophobic people who want all homosexuals to fit their own unpleasant images. Their perception of who you are is their reality, not yours. It is important for you to dress and behave in accordance with your own values and in ways that make you feel comfortable. *The lesbian, gay, and bisexual community is as diverse as any other, and the community celebrates this diversity.*

IS THERE ANYONE I CAN LOOK UP TO?

Yes! Like never before, lesbians, gays, and bisexuals are coming out, becoming involved in the community, being visible, and being heard. Many famous people are gay:

entertainers such as Melissa Etheridge, Elton John, k.d. lang, and Lily Tomlin; athletes such as Greg Louganis, the Olympic gold medal diver, and Martina Navratilova, the tennis champion; political leaders such as Massachusetts representatives Barney Frank and Gerry Studds, and Wisconsin representative Steve Gunderson.

The list goes on and on. You'll also run across gay, lesbian, and bisexual people in all of your school subjects. History? Remember Alexander the Great, the Macedonian king and conqueror of Persia; or Susan B. Anthony, pioneer feminist and organizer of the National Women's Suffrage Movement; or Sir Richard Burton, the British explorer. Literature? There's Walt Whitman, the founder of modern American poetry; Gertrude Stein, the famous poet and novelist who lived with her partner Alice B. Toklas; E. M. Forster, Virginia Woolf, Willa Cather, and James Baldwin, to name a few. Music wouldn't be the same without Peter Ilyich Tchaikovsky or Leonard Bernstein. Probably if you are taught about these people in school, there will be no mention of their sexual orientation. What is important is that all of these people and many, many others made contributions both to the world and to the history of lesbians, gays, and bisexuals.

You don't have to look just to famous people for role models. There are people to look up to in all communities and all areas: politics, the arts, the environment, education, sports, medicine, human services, religion. Role models also come in all sexual orientations. It's important to know that so many different people offer their values and strengths to society as a whole as well as to the lesbian, gay, and bisexual community.

These questions mark the beginning of the road to discovering and accepting your sexual orientation—and yourself. As you read through this book, we hope you will find the answers to your questions and where to get the additional information and support you need. We also hope you will feel free to share this book with friends, family, teachers, or anyone else who is important to you. You don't have to be alone when you hit the road.

CHAPTER TWO

THE JOURNEY TO SELF-ACCEPTANCE

"I did have trouble accepting myself. I thought I would change and be normal." —Andie, 17

"I was 16 when I figured out who I was. The first second I knew, I was relieved, and the next minute I freaked out." —Gretchen, 18

"You know how you can know something without really knowing why or how? I just always knew that I was gay and I never thought I wasn't okay. Then I told my folks and they didn't make a big deal out of it. So I feel pretty good about my life in general." —Marc, 17

Marc is fortunate. It would be wonderful if his experience was echoed by all lesbian, gay, and bisexual people's journeys to self-acceptance. That's what we would wish for all teens embarking on the various roads to self-discovery. But these first years on the road are rarely easy ones. This is a time when much of the knowledge you will gain about yourself will be simultaneously exciting and scary, joyous and distressing, empowering and mystifying.

Just being a teen is full of surprises. Your body is undergoing a variety of changes, thanks to those hormonal rushes, and your mind is busy keeping pace. You want to do well in school and get good grades and you want to fit into the social scene. You want your family to be proud of you, and at the same time you want to start making your own decisions. One day you're on a reasonably even keel, the next day something sends you into a funk. One day you are busy thinking about your first date and that night the largest pimple known to medical science appears on your chin! The following day, you are chosen for the tennis team and your joy and self-esteem soar. Rest assured that gay or straight, Jewish or Christian, Latino or African-American, Asian-American or Caucasian, you are not alone as you go through the mood swings and mind shifts, the milestones on the road through your teen years.

You may or may not be sure that you are gay. Not knowing is part of the process for some teens. A few do not need much reflection; one day they just wake up and say, "aha!" Everyone is different, and your eventual self-acceptance can depend on a variety of factors: your general self-esteem, how well you cope with difficult issues, what you've learned about lesbian, gay, and bisexual people over the years, whether or not you've had the support of your family, the willingness of your friends to be there for you, and your ability to recognize when to get help.

Discovering that you might be lesbian, gay, or bisexual is very much like waking up in the morning. Some of us leap out of bed, ready to start the day. Others yawn and try to go back to sleep until the final alarm gets them going. Others stretch mightily and poke one foot out from under the covers tentatively, a little unsure, and not quite ready to deal with what's out there. Still others, in complete denial of the dawning of a new day, sleep blissfully through the music, the alarm, and a friend's wake-up call.

Indeed, recognition of your sexuality *is* an awakening. It's your awakening to yet another aspect of yourself. "Well," you may say, "I'm a reasonable person. Is this like being left-handed or having to wear glasses? I can handle that."

Yes. And no.

Being left-handed, like being gay, is something you were born with, along with your tendency to being near- or farsighted. It may have taken time to adapt to being left-handed, since most tools are made for right-handed people. As for wearing glasses, it probably did take a while for you to adjust to having them sitting on your nose, slipping down, leaving a mark on the bridge of your nose, until you and your eye doctor made adjustments to them so they fit. Both adaptations took time and patience, just as being gay does.

But the recognition of your sexual orientation won't be as clear-cut. It could be tentative: "I think I might be gay—but maybe I'm not." It's okay not to know for sure. It's also okay to read as much as you can about the subject, talk to a close friend that you trust, attend a support group, call a gay telephone rap line, or join a conversation on the electronic communication highway. These are only some of the resources available to help you gain more knowledge about yourself. It is important to know that you are not alone in your uncertainty.

Here's another type of recognition: "I'm pretty sure I'm gay even though I sometimes deny it to myself. I sure wish I could feel good about it all the time. After all, it's just another part of me, isn't it?"

Absolutely—it is another part of you. Recent scientific research has uncovered compelling evidence that being gay is at least partly hereditary. In 1993, a team of researchers at the Laboratory of Biochemistry of the National Cancer Institute (NCI) discovered that pairs of gay brothers shared specific genetic material (the part of you that controls the characteristics you inherit from your parents). Just as there are genes that determine eye and hair color, there seem to be genes that are associated with being gay. (This study focused on gay men; the NCI team's study of lesbians is in progress as of this writing, though early results point to the existence of a "lesbian gene," as well.) To deny your sexual orientation doesn't just keep you from accepting yourself, it makes about as much sense as denying your eye color. *Accepting yourself is the most important thing you will ever do.* It's a gift you will give yourself over and over again.

You have to decide from the time you recognize the possibility of your being lesbian, gay, or bisexual just how you will accomplish this acceptance. Everyone's journey is unique and ongoing. As we said earlier, self-acceptance is a continual process. And there is no magic wand anyone can wave over your head to make it easier, much as they might wish to. People at school and work, family, and peers can all help you. And sometimes, sadly, they can also take a bite out of your self-esteem and the way you feel about yourself.

"Well, just when I was on the road to liking this part of me—you know, accepting it, I heard this creep on the street say, 'Get out of the way, faggot!'" recalls one teen. "I got so mad at him. Then I was mad at myself. I wanted to hit him. Later I wanted to beat up on myself."

Sometimes others' perceptions of you are grossly unfair or totally wrong. Frequently, young people grow up hearing homophobic messages from family, church, the media, strangers, and even from friends. These messages can challenge and alter the way you feel about yourself. You want to be accepted by others. Even more important, you want to be proud of your accomplishments and grow up with a sense of self-esteem, with the ability to move forward in your life. This feeling is challenged every time you are faced with harassment or negative feedback. A rotten comment made by someone you know, or even someone you don't know, can feel like a huge blow to your self-worth. It may make you want to take a step backward and ask yourself, "Why me?"

But try the question another way: not "why *me*?" but "why *them*?" Consider who is giving you this negative response, and why. Friends, family, and strangers on the street—anyone might have some homophobic feelings, some irrational fears about gay people. These feelings can come from ignorance, a value system that is different from yours, false assumptions, anger and hate, or the too-human need to find a scapegoat for life's difficulties. It would be wonderful if this was an ideal world and such fears could be dispelled with reason and understanding. But we can't hope to change people's minds so easily. Just remember that homophobia is in their minds—it doesn't have to be in yours.

Internalized homophobia, a gay person's fear of being gay, is another issue. Many things can bring this about, and it can take many forms. People may attempt to disprove their homosexuality by behaving in a "heterosexual" manner, even participating in gay-bashing. Some turn homophobia inward, hurting themselves with high-risk behavior and self-destructive habits such as drugs and alcohol abuse. Internalized homophobia is a serious issue, one we'll explore more in Chapter 6. It shouldn't be confused with self-doubt, something that is perfectly natural and affects everyone at various points in life.

Self-doubt is a funny thing. It can creep in just as easily when things are going well as when they're not. That doubt may affect how you see yourself in relation to school, your family, your peers, and sometimes your community. Max, 16, says, "Sometimes I get it from my pastor when he quotes from the Bible about sin. I feel like he's picking me out from the crowd. I wish I could tell him that I've tried to change. I would never hurt anyone. I've tried to date girls—I don't feel anything when I kiss a girl. I'm so lonely. It's not that I want to have sex with anyone; I'm not ready for that yet. But I would sure like to talk to someone like me."

Think about Max. Someone he has listened to all of his life, someone he's probably respected, has given Max reason to doubt himself. Because he is feeling lonely as well, he is at an extremely vulnerable time in his life. Sound familiar?

Max is beginning to question his sexuality, as many

young people do. Max may need to talk to a teacher, counselor, trusted family member, or friend, someone who will acknowledge his concerns and help him deal with his self-doubts. Perhaps Max needs to question what his religion is really saying and to reconcile his faith with what he is discovering about himself. Balancing the demands of personal faith and organized religion can be tricky, as we will see. To understand and resolve his doubts about his religion, or any other aspect of his evolving self, Max needs to consider his basic values.

Regardless of sexual orientation, all teens are reconsidering their values—those they've been taught and those they have learned on their own. Discovering that you might be gay won't change most of these values. It won't make you suddenly a bad person—or a good one. If your values include excelling in your studies, in sports, or in other activities, and helping others and yourself, then you'll do great!

The negative messages young people receive from the outside world can be hurtful and daunting. They can cause you to lose courage on your journey. Being gay in this world is still a struggle. Becoming comfortable with who you are is the best way to deal with this struggle. Your acceptance of yourself is your most powerful tool in dealing with the obstacles that may be put in your way— one that will be with you for the rest of your life.

There will be times when you are challenged not only

by others, but by yourself as well. You may be your most severe critic: "I hate my nose, I hate my hair, I hate my laugh, and now I'm gay." Sometimes you will take steps backward when you want to be moving forward. Getting to know yourself is *not* always love at first sight.

Sophie, now 25, says:

As I look back on my teen years, I realize that it wasn't always easy to respect and love myself. It took a long time to truly believe that I was a good person. There were so many others who disapproved of my being a lesbian. I had to keep telling myself that I have wonderful qualities. I am a good friend to my friends; I work well with others. I care about my family. I have a good heart. I volunteer at the Pediatric AIDS unit of our local childrens' hospital. Being a lesbian and having faced oppression most of my life has helped me grow to be an empathetic, caring, and loving person. Loving myself came when I was able to put my sexual orientation into perspective.

Learning to love and respect yourself, even when part of your basic nature is not respected by the outside world, is the key to your personal journey. No matter how great friends, parents, or peers think you are, they can't give you this quality. *You* have to put the "self" in front of re-spect. That will come from knowing and accepting yourself—your total self. Even when it's a bad test day, a bad hair day, or a bad creep-on-the-street day, if in general you feel good about yourself, you won't let it (or them) get to you. It's how you see yourself that matters.

Greg, now 26, says:

The road was tough when I was younger. It's still diffi-cult at times. My self-acceptance and self-respect have gone up and down depending on where I was in my life. In high school, for instance, the other students made fun of me and I was beaten up twice, although I wasn't out to anyone. At college, I felt more comfortable with myself. By then I was pretty much out and I was also active in the gay and lesbian student alliance on campus. It was im-portant to me for my parents to understand, and today we have a good relationship. I've also found a wonderful man to love. I have a good job with a national company but after I worked there for a while I realized that I was one of only a few gay employees. I started to question whether I should come out at work or if I could even take my partner to company functions. For now, since it's a new job, I'm not out at work. I realize that life is going to be full of times when I ask questions like these and occa-sionally get discouraged. Then I remember who I am—a productive member of society who is also gay. And that's how I get through the tough times.

Finding out about yourself and accepting who you are takes courage and time; time for your self-acceptance to grow, time to feel comfortable with yourself. Sometimes you will find the path you have embarked on stressful and even painful. But the rewards can be great, as Sophie and Greg and others like them have discovered. When you find out who you are and what you need, you will also find out how much you have to give others.

CHAPTER THREE

I THINK I HAVE
SOMETHING TO TELL YOU . . .

"My mother was the first person I told, because I trust her and we are very close—we've always been close. Even though there have been times that we didn't get along, we managed to work things out. I consider my mother my best friend." —Asha, 16

"When I came out to my folks, at first they were in shock. In a couple of days I was able to talk to my mom; I think she was trying to understand. But then my father came out of his shock—he hadn't said one word to me since I told them. He shouted some terrible things—he said that I was no son of his. He made me pack my stuff into my backpack

and told me I had to get out. He didn't want me contaminating my younger brothers."

—Kent, 15

Self-acceptance, as we've said, is a continuous process, and of critical importance when you decide to come out. How comfortable you feel with your sexual orientation, what you've learned about homosexuality, and the timing of your announcement are also important. If you are experiencing feelings of guilt, anger, or fear about your sexual identity being "uncovered," then this may not be the time to come out. If you feel you are ready, there are some important things to consider about whom you tell and how you tell them.

TELLING PARENTS

Before you make the decision to tell your parents, there are a number of questions to consider:

▼ How comfortable are you with your sexual orientation?
▼ How well do you know your parents?
▼ How has your family dealt with political, religious, cultural, and social issues in the past?
▼ How close are you to your parents?
▼ Is the timing right to come out?

▼ Are you economically and emotionally dependent on your parents?

▼ How safe are you in your home?

▼ Do you have a support system for yourself?

▼ How much information do you have, and are you able to share it with your parents?

Try to answer these questions as honestly as possible, and remember: it is imperative to look at your parents as objectively as you can before you make the decision to come out to them.

Knowing Your Parents

Parents come in all sizes, shapes, and mind-sets. Some parents may have strong opinions and will not tolerate argument. Others pride themselves on being reasonable and understanding. Or they may be a combination of the two. Parents may be politically liberal, conservative, or middle-of-the-road. Your parents may be people you trust, people you've shared your feelings with, people who laugh with you rather than at you—or they may be people who have hurt you in the past, people you love but have learned to not always trust with personal matters. All parents are different, and only you can know if you'll be able to talk to them safely about your sexual orientation.

From years of talking with and listening to your

parents, you can be reasonably sure where they stand on political and social issues such as abortion, health care, women's rights, welfare, and so on. You've probably also had discussions about personal issues such as dating, friends, or your education. As their child, you have listened to and learned their values over the years, and have picked up on the clear or subtle expectations they have for you. If you have older brothers or sisters, you've seen these issues come up and seen how your parents have dealt with them. Brothers and sisters can help you figure out—directly or indirectly—how your parents might respond to certain issues. If you have good family dynamics, with all members of the family playing a role in family debates and decisions, they can help you come out when you are ready.

Timing

Once you've decided to talk to your parents, think about how best to time your announcement. James, 17, was ready to tell his parents one night at dinner, "Mom, Dad, I want to talk to you about being gay."

But his parents had another family concern at that moment: James's mother had just learned that she had a lump in her breast. That was the only important topic of discussion that evening and for many weeks afterwards while the family saw her through her surgery and recovery. While James had to put aside his declaration temporarily, he eventually found the right time to talk to his parents.

Laura, nearly 18, was about to graduate from high school and had plans to attend a fairly expensive, out-of-state college. Her decision not to tell her parents about her sexual orientation was based on a pragmatic, and some might say, selfish rationale. Even though she had a part-time job to help pay her way through college, she did not want to risk losing the money she and her parents had put away for her education. Sol Gordon, Ph.D., an internationally respected author on the subject of teen sexuality, says in his book, *When Living Hurts*, "You may want to wait until you are eighteen and in college. Even then it's not easy."

You may also want to consider the impact of coming out during a holiday. Getting together to celebrate holidays can be stressful for some family members, and it's a good idea to choose a time to tell that isn't stressful in itself.

After carefully considering all the family variables, you may find that now is not the time to come out to your parents. It's okay to wait. People and circumstances change, and your best time to tell might still be in the future.

Another option is to open the door slightly, asking for help from your parents without giving any specifics. For example, Ann, 16, told her mother, "Mom, I am going through a lot of stuff right now that I can't talk about. I would like to see a therapist. Maybe later I can let you know what's going on." This may be a prelude to coming out to your parents at a later date.

Safety

If timing is all, safety is *everything*! As Stefani, 20, says, "It was safe for me to come out because I am all I have. I thought it was safe when I became comfortable enough with my own sexuality that it didn't matter what anyone else thought. But I believe a young person should stay in the closet if they think they will be verbally, mentally, or physically abused."

If your family has a history of violence—verbal, mental, physical, or sexual abuse—they are not the people you want to come out to. *Just get help immediately.* The people you need in your life at this point are those who can help you deal with the abuse in addition to coming-out issues. Abuse is not a coming-out issue, but it is an extremely serious issue for your mental and physical safety. It's important when considering your safety to have a support system in place before you come out. A support system may be a counselor or therapist, teacher or member of the clergy, or a close friend or family member. A family member might even surprise you (remember that "gay gene").

You can also seek support from a lesbian and gay community center in your area. (See the Resources section in the back of the book to find the center nearest you.) Most centers have counseling services and support groups for young people dealing with the process of coming out. All groups and services are confidential; you don't even have to use your real name. Nor do you have to worry that walking into a community center automatically commits you to a gay, lesbian, or bisexual orientation. Centers are as welcoming to people who are questioning their sexuality as they are to the gay community. Many also offer support groups and counseling for parents of lesbians, gays, and bisexuals.

Information

Knowledge will set you free. Do your homework about sexual orientation, the lesbian, gay, and bisexual community, and local support groups. You should be prepared to give your parents the best information you can find at the time you plan to begin the discussion. There are many books, videos, and magazines that can help. One of the best books for parents is *Now That You Know*, by Betty Fairchild and Nancy Hayward. There are also support groups for parents that will help them understand the coming-out journey. Parents, Families and Friends of Lesbians and Gays (PFLAG) is an excellent resource for parents and their children.

What to Expect

In the best-case scenario, your parents' first reaction might be: "You are my child and I love you," or "I am glad you were able to tell me. I sort of suspected, but I didn't know for sure." Many parents respond with love and compassion—if not right away, in time. But it is best to be prepared for a variety of reactions, even from parents who want to understand and be supportive. Responses can include:

▼ Shock: No one will say anything. This could lead into . . .

▼ Denial: "No, I don't believe it." "Don't you think this could just be a phase you are going through?"

▼ Anger: "Do you know what this is going to do to your grandparents [or brothers, or sisters, etc.]?" "How could you make such a stupid decision?" "Don't think for a minute you are going to be gay and live under my roof."

▼ Grief: "You'll never be happy." "I'll never have grandchildren."

▼ Guilt: "What did I do to deserve this?" "What did I do wrong?" "It's all my fault."

▼ Bargaining or pleading: "Please just try to be straight for me." "I know this nice girl/boy. Won't you just call her/him?" "If we go pray together this will go away."

Your parents could go through any or all of these emotional states. But they are all a manifestation of the same thing: mourning the loss of the child they thought they knew. These responses are all stages in the process of grieving and eventual acceptance. The high expectations your parents had for their child are replaced by sadness at the thought of the pain and harassment they believe you will experience by being homosexual in a predominantly heterosexual world. It is a loss and sorrow that your parents may have no name for, a feeling they may or may not be able to resolve. Loss is a very intense emotion. They may feel almost as if the you they thought they knew so well has died and been replaced by a stranger. You, too, may have felt this way and gone through your own process of grieving, mourning the loss of your childhood and learning to accept yourself as a sexual being.

Some parents will take time to go through the stages of accepting loss and then become very supportive. Others will get stuck in one or more of the stages for a period of time. A few will never be able to move to a reasonable resolution. It will take time and patience for you and your parents to come to an understanding and acceptance of your sexual orientation. Your parents may want or need support from you at the same time that you are desperate for their support. They, too, may need to talk things over with a counselor or therapist.

Not all parents who have an immediate strong negative

reaction will continue to feel this way. One mother ran into the bathroom and threw up when her son told her that he was gay. But then she returned, hugged him, and told him how much she loved him. She is now his greatest ally and has helped other family members and friends come to terms with their feelings.

Some parents may listen to what you have to say once, and never want to discuss it again. It may seem that they have digested what you told them, but in reality they are angry or in denial. "What you do in your free time is your business, but I don't want it in my home and I don't ever want to talk about it. And don't bring any of your new friends home with you." If this is their response, you will want to seek support from your friends, other family members, or an outside group. Sometimes a relative can be an unexpected ally. Grace recalls, "My grandmother was the first person I decided to come out to. We'd always been very close. I was so nervous when I said, 'Nan, I think I'm gay.' But then she shot back, 'Well, I'm bi, you know.' "

If, after you have explained who you are and what you are feeling to the best of your abilities, and after you have given your parents time to work out their own feelings, they still refuse to accept you, you may need to give the subject a rest. Make sure you have other people in your life who will give you support. Meanwhile, don't push your parents out of your life. Love them. Teach them if you can. Leave the avenues of communication open. They may come to you when they're ready.

If your parents continue to be angry and they are hurting you—emotionally or physically—consider your own safety. If you believe that you are in danger, seek help from professionals or social service agencies. There are places to turn to for individual or family counseling and mediation between young people and their families. If you feel you are no longer safe at home, or, in the worst-case scenario, if your parents kick you out, there are organizations in every state in the United States and in many other countries that can provide you with counseling, food, and housing. Some gay community centers also offer foster-care placement programs or shelters for young people in need of housing. They can help you find a home with supportive adults, where you can complete your education, find a job, and become self-sufficient. Centers can also help connect you with the various agencies that serve homeless and disenfranchised youth. You must not put yourself in further danger by living on the streets or taking the pain and rejection you are feeling out on yourself. "Jay," who did not want his real name used, can tell you what that is like.

Jay was kicked out of his home when he was thirteen. He has lived with foster parents—and he's lived in a dumpster. For a time, he supported himself by prostitution. In the beginning, he admits that hustling was also a way to come out, and part of his desperate search for affection. He continued to hustle for a living even while he attended classes to get his Graduate Equivalency Diploma, trying to move on to a better life. Now 20, Jay is HIV positive, unsure whether he picked up the virus from his off-and-on use of heroin or from hustling. "I'm trying to get my act together," Jay says with a shy grin. "I lose it sometimes—then I come back. I'm a survivor."

TELLING PEERS AND FRIENDS

"I knew I could trust and be open with my friends. I didn't feel that way about my family. I find it easier to tell my friends when I am alone with them rather than in a crowd." —Amber, 16

"I told a friend because she asked and I hoped I could trust her. Instead, she told her sister who spread it all over the school." —Kevin, 18

Sometimes it's easier and less threatening to come out to a friend than to your family. Your friends may be less judgmental. Of course, using common sense about whom you tell, and when and how you tell them, is critical. Sometimes peers and even friends can be surprisingly insensitive. Sometimes they can be just plain jerks. Remember, your friends are dealing with their own sexuality too, and they may feel threatened by revelations about yours.

Whom Do You Tell?

Every person you tell should be someone you have shared secrets with and who has a good track record in keeping them—a trustworthy friend who understands the importance of your privacy and values your safety and well-being. And of course it should not be someone who makes disparaging remarks about lesbians, gays, and bisexuals. By telling the wrong person, you may leave yourself open to verbal or physical harassment by peers, schoolmates, even school staff.

When and Where Should You Tell Your Friends?

Again, use common sense in this decision. Telling people in the middle of the cafeteria, only to hear them shout at the top of their lungs, "You're queer?" may put you in danger. As with parents, timing is everything. You may want to practice coming out to peers at a lesbian, gay, and bisexual support group, joining in role-playing games, acting out the how, when, and where of telling your friends. You can also simply practice the words by yourself, planning what you want to say or writing out different scenarios.

How Do You Tell Your Friends?

Often telling a friend in an open, straightforward fashion is the best way. For example: "Megan, I think we are close enough that you should know more about me. I am a lesbian. I know that this may really freak you out, or maybe you're okay with it. Either way, I need to trust that you won't tell anyone, at least not yet." Your friend may surprise you with the best response of all: "No big deal; I sort of guessed." Or she or he may respond with questions: "How do you know you're gay?" "Are you telling me because you think I'm gay?" "How do you know for sure if you haven't had sex?" "Can we still be friends?"

How you respond to these questions depends on your relationship with your friend and how comfortable you feel talking about your sexuality. If your friend does not understand, she or he may be going through the same emotional stages mentioned in the section on telling parents: shock, denial, anger, grief, guilt, and bargaining or pleading. Giving friends time, information, and the assurance that you don't want this to hurt your friendship can help them through this process.

If telling other people doesn't work out the way you want, don't despair. Telling others, like self-acceptance, is part of the journey. It can give you support when you most need it and answer questions you have about yourself—or it can give you a whole new set of questions and issues to consider. And maybe, as with Ann, 16, telling will take a relationship to whole new level. Ann's grandmother didn't just support her—she marched with her in the Gay Pride parade!

CHAPTER FOUR

COULD THIS BE LOVE?

"I thought the process of coming out was getting a girlfriend."   —*Liz, 18*

"I am a true romantic: I don't want to get involved or have sex until I find my Romeo."
               —*Tim, 19*

Your growing awareness of your sexual orientation can be a personal, private discovery process. It can take time to meet the right person and time before you are ready for an intimate relationship.

First love can also be part of the coming-out process, a validation of your homosexuality. It could start with a crush on a same-sex friend. Your speech falters and you feel yourself blush when you are close to your friend.

Your stomach flip-flops, your tongue ties itself in knots. Maybe you want to shout from a mountaintop, "Yeah! I finally know what I've been feeling all this time." These emotions can be startling, exhilarating, and frightening all at once.

The recognition and return of these emotional or sexual feelings by another person may be the fulfillment of all your wishes. You may want to throw yourself completely into this first love, believing it will last forever on such a high note.

First love is always very special and always a learning and growing experience. In the beginning it may be fun sneaking around as two against the world. You may both be as much attracted to the idea of your first close relationship as to each other. But relationships are always in a state of flux, as you both change, and grow. This makes it important to evaluate your roles and values and the goals of your relationship after that first heady excitement wears off. And believe it or not, it does wear off; your body and mind can't keep up that high pitch of excitement forever!

HEALTHY AND UNHEALTHY RELATIONSHIPS

Relationships have different meanings for different people. People find each other, fall in love, or form close attachments for a variety of reasons. Sometimes these

reasons are healthy—sometimes not. A loving relationship with another person is based on your relationship
with yourself and your sensitivity to your own and other
people's needs, as well as other loving relationships you
have seen or experienced.

Amber, 16, who is now in a good relationship, recalls,
"At first there was a constant need or pressure to make
sure I was giving enough and not taking too much. After
we learned to balance that out, we have been in a healthy
relationship. We communicate, we're honest, and most of
all, we trust each other."

Roger, 20, says, "When I first came out I believed that
good sex made a good relationship. I know I went crazy
and did some really stupid things. All I wanted was acceptance and love. I thought I had to have sex to find it. I
learned some tough lessons then."

Everyone approaches relationships in a different way,
and every relationship has its ups and downs. There is no
scientific formula for finding lifelong love. Healthy and
lasting relationships do have certain things in common,
though.

Consider whether you and your girlfriend or boy-
friend:

▼ Share common interests
▼ Are both reasonably comfortable with your sex-
    ual orientation

39

▼ Have common values
▼ Can communicate and laugh together
▼ Respect each other as individuals
▼ Support and nurture each other
▼ Are equal partners in your relationship
▼ Are not dependent solely on the other person
▼ Are willing to work together through any difficulties and get outside support together if needed

You will probably find that the two of you already do some of these things, though you shouldn't expect everything to come together in one fell swoop! Relationships are works in progress. If, however, too many of these elements are missing, it could be time for you and your partner to take a long, hard look at where your relationship is going. Talk things out. Real communication is one of the most important things that holds a relationship together.

There are good times and bad times in even the best relationships. But if all or most of the times are bad, you could be in an unhealthy relationship. Some signs of an unhealthy relationship are:

▼ One partner's total emotional, financial, and spiritual dependency on the other
▼ Constant jealousy and suspicion
▼ Uncontrollable anger or rage

▼ Obsessive love: one partner's life totally revolving around the other, which raises the risk of the relationship becoming abusive

▼ Lack of communication or constant miscommunication

▼ Giving without receiving in return, or taking without giving

▼ Unresolvable insensitivity to or intolerance of each other's needs or beliefs

▼ Laughter and fun and good times spent together stopping

▼ Verbal, physical, or sexual abuse

In general, a relationship becomes violent or abusive when another person treats you as a possession or needs to control you. When this occurs, don't try fixing the relationship or making excuses. There's only one way to change the dynamics of the situation: *get out*! Find a counselor, crisis hot line, teacher, member of the clergy, support group, parent, or friend to help you during this crisis. If you feel your safety is threatened, protect yourself. Get a restraining order with the help of an attorney, someone from an anti-violence project, or another adult. This will not be easy. But you must not allow yourself to be mistreated! By empowering yourself to get help and by removing yourself from an abusive relationship, you will strengthen your resolve never to be in this situation again.

Sometimes when a relationship hurts, it can be fixed, either by talking things through or seeking outside help. Sometimes you know in your heart that it must end. At other times, particularly if your sense of identity or self-esteem are low, you will make excuses for the pain in your relationship. You may not even be aware that you are doing this, though friends and family members may pick up on it. Listen to what people outside your relationship, people you trust, have to say. It could be time to seek help for yourself, and to know that loving and nurturing yourself is even more important than fixing the relationship.

A good relationship can give you so much. It helps provide validation and acceptance of your sexual orientation. You share affection and perhaps intimacy. You believe that someone loves you for who you are. And you love someone in return. When a relationship ends, grieving for the loss of all this is natural.

Allow yourself the time to process all the mixed emotions you may have: anger, isolation, fear, hurt, even relief. Whether you have left the relationship or have been left, a time for reflection is important now. The healing process can also be a time for rediscovering and redefining yourself as an individual. Keeping a journal, talking to a good friend and participating in activities with your friends or peers, going to a support group or seeing a counselor are all positive steps. Thinking about the qualities you liked or disliked about the relationship or the person are ways to come to an understanding of why the breakup occurred.

Naturally it's easier to blame the other person for the breakup. But you will find it more rewarding in the end to be honest with yourself and try to come to an understanding of your own behavior and feelings in the relationship. Do not spend too much time alone. And don't look for immediate gratification in another relationship during your grieving period. It would be just a small Band-Aid for a large wound.

Each relationship helps you to grow, to learn what you need and want from others—and what you can offer yourself as well as other people. It is said that all those we have loved become a part of us. Even when love relationships fail, something from that person remains, helping you to understand yourself and how you relate to others. Put another, less romantic way, "Whatever doesn't kill me makes me stronger." Love with your heart *and* your head and you'll find strength. But first, of course, you have to find someone to love!

How Do You Meet Other Lesbians, Gays, and Bisexuals?

Gay or straight, meeting other young people can be difficult. Finding that one special person can be a lifelong process. For lesbians, gays, and bisexuals, it is especially difficult because you don't always know who is gay and who is straight. Some homosexuals claim to have "gaydar," a built-in radar that picks up on subtle signals, telling them when someone else is gay. There is no scientific backing for this phenomenon, and no denying that it is real. It all comes down to trusting your instincts.

Lesbian, gay, and bisexual people are everywhere in mainstream society. You may find them in your math class, photography club, or on the softball team at school. You can also meet other gay people through community centers. These offer gay support groups and provide space for meetings and sponsor such events as gay socials, rap sessions, movie nights, and dances or "under 21" nights at gay bars, where alcohol is not served. All types of people attend these social events. They come from every race, religion, and economic class, some in school, some working, some living at home, and others out on their own. Some will be confident about who they are and have experience with relationships. Others will be uncertain about their sexuality and terrified of making a date. The one thing you can be sure of finding at a center social is that you're not alone.

In many places you'll find there is a gay subculture within the larger culture. In large cities there are often neighborhoods with stores, coffee houses, and restaurants which cater to a gay clientele. There are rallies and marches, gay sport teams, choirs, dancing and acting groups, even gay rodeos.

Many cities and states have their own gay and lesbian yellow pages, often free of charge, which list community centers, restaurants, stores, and so on that are gay-owned or gay-friendly. These can be found in gay and non-gay bookstores, community centers, or libraries, or by calling PFLAG. Or check the Resource section in the back of this book for places to call about meeting other young people.

Don't give up the everyday activities you enjoy, such as sports, music, or church groups. Valuable friendships grow from common interests—and you never know where friendship might lead!

CHAPTER FIVE

COMING TO TERMS WITH THE TERMS

"I hate it when people who don't know me shout 'fag' at me on the street or in school. But when I'm with a group at the teen center, we joke among ourselves and it's okay then. Why can't I get used to it in the outside world?" —Lewis, 17

"Why must there be labels? When did I stop being a teen and become something else: a curse word? I have a name like everybody else!"

—Dina, 14

What's in a name? A lot more than you might expect! Take the words "dyke" and "fag." A homophobic person might use those words to hurt you, while a gay person might use them to refer to his or her gay friends, taking the sting out of the hurtful words by making them a joke. Another gay person might never use the words, working to eliminate them from the common vocabulary altogether.

There is a lot of debate within the gay community about which terms are "politically correct," that is, which words make a positive statement about gay people and the gay community. The debate is ongoing, and the issues are complex. We can't resolve them here, but we can give you a "queer" primer, so you can join in the debate.

ANDROGYNOUS: Having both feminine and masculine feelings and exhibiting both "masculine" and "feminine" behaviors. This term is used regardless of gender or sexual orientation.

BISEXUAL: A man or woman who is affectionally and sexually attracted to both men and woman. A bisexual can be attracted more strongly to one gender than to the other, or be attracted equally to both.

BUTCH: A gay man or lesbian who looks traditionally "masculine"; used for "masculine" dress or behavior, regardless of sexual orientation.

COMING OUT: A metaphor for the act of telling others that you are lesbian, gay, or bisexual; "the coming out process," refers to the steps by which lesbians, gays, and bisexuals come to accept their sexual orientation.

IN THE CLOSET: An allusion to a lesbian, gay, or bisexual who, for whatever reason, has hidden his or her sexual orientation from family, friends, acquaintances, and society in general. Homosexuals and bisexuals who are open about their sexual orientation are "out of the closet."

CROSS-DRESSER: A woman who dresses as a man or a man who dresses as a woman. Cross-dressers, like *transvestites,* are not necessarily homosexuals; straight men and women also cross-dress.

DRAG QUEEN: A gay man who dresses as a woman for the entertainment of others or for fun.

DYKE: A lesbian, usually used in reference to a "masculine" lesbian. The word is often used as a homophobic taunt, though lesbians themselves now use it as a friendly, joking way to refer to themselves and their friends.

FAG or FAGGOT: A gay man. As with "dyke," this can be used as a taunt, or as a term of affection among gay men. "Faggot" literally means "bundle of sticks" and is believed to have first been applied to homosexuals during the Spanish Inquisition, when gay men were burned at the stake for their "crimes."

FAG HAG: A heterosexual woman who prefers the company of gay men. The term can be either derogative or affectionate.

FEMALE IMPERSONATOR: A man, gay or straight, who emulates and imitates the physical appearance, voice, attitude, and actions of women as a form of theatrical entertainment.

FEMME: A lesbian who exhibits "feminine" characteristics. Another term is lipstick lesbian.

FREEDOM RINGS: Rainbow colored rings worn as a sign of gay pride and the diversity of the gay community. They are modeled on the *rainbow flag*.

GAY: Homosexual, most often used to refer to a man. "Gay" can also be used to describe the entire homosexual community, including both men and women (see also *queer*). In the United Kingdom, "bent" (as opposed to "straight") is more common.

HETEROSEXUAL: The formal term describing someone who has affectionate and sexual feelings for members of the opposite gender.

HETEROSEXISM: The false assumption that everyone is or should be heterosexual because it is the only acceptable and viable orientation. This assumption often leads to *homophobia* and discrimination.

HOMOPHOBIA: The irrational fear, dislike, or hatred of lesbians, gays, and bisexuals. Homophobia can be both a personal and an institutionalized prejudice.

HOMOSEXUAL: The formal term describing someone

who has affectionate and sexual feelings for members of the same gender.

LABRYS: A symbol of lesbian strength and pride, based on the double-bladed battle-ax believed to be used by the legendary Greek Amazons and their goddess.

LAMBDA: The Greek letter λ, adopted in 1970 by the Gay Activists Alliance in New York City to represent the gay movement.

LESBIAN: A homosexual woman. The term is derived from the Greek island of Lesbos, where the poet Sappho had her academy, circa 400 B.C.

LIFE PARTNER: A "spouse" in a committed lesbian, gay, or bisexual relationship; also called "companion" or "lover."

LIPSTICK LESBIAN: See *Femme*.

OUTING: Exposing someone's homosexuality or bisexuality without that person's consent.

PINK TRIANGLE: An inverted pink triangle worn by lesbians, gays, and bisexuals as a symbol of pride, and in remembrance of the thousands of homosexuals killed in concentration camps by the Nazis during World War II. All prisoners in the concentration camps wore symbols representing their "crimes"; the pink triangle was the symbol assigned to homosexuals.

QUEEN: A gay man who exhibits feminine behavior;

the term can, but does not necessarily, refer to someone who cross-dresses.

QUEER: A term used by the homosexual and bisexual community to refer to themselves. Because "queer" is often a derogative term used by heterosexuals, this use is a particular subject of debate.

RAINBOW FLAG: The six-striped, multi-colored flag designed in 1978 by Gilbert Baker for the San Francisco Gay Freedom Day parade representing the diversity of the lesbian, gay, and bisexual community.

SEXUAL ORIENTATION: A classification of sexual identity ranging from homosexual (feeling attraction and affection toward members of your own sex) to bisexual (having these feelings toward both sexes) to heterosexual (having these feelings toward members of the opposite sex).

STRAIGHT: A heterosexual or non-gay person.

TRANSSEXUAL: A person who feels that her or his biological gender is not her or his real gender. A transsexual may seek surgical or hormonal treatment to alter his or her gender.

TRANSVESTITE: A person who wears clothing or makeup which is socially considered to be more appropriate for the opposite gender. Transvestites are not necessarily homosexual.

CHAPTER SIX

TO YOUR HEALTH

Both gay and straight young people often feel that they are immune to major health problems: they're too old for childhood diseases, and too young to think about degenerative diseases. Guess again. Now is the time to start thinking seriously about your health. Disease and ill health can strike anytime and anyone, regardless of sexuality. Gay teens, however, do have a higher susceptibility to stress-related disorders. The process of discovering and accepting your sexual orientation can be difficult, and you should take care that your mental and physical health don't suffer. Developing good health-care habits and knowing about health issues now will help ensure continued good health for the rest of your life.

You can start by maintaining a regular exercise schedule and following good nutritional habits. The occasional Twinkie or burger binge won't do you any harm. Just remember that the four basic food groups are not chocolate, caffeine, soda, and cigarettes.

Actually, cigarettes are a whole different issue. It may be tempting to try smoking; it may look glamorous and hip. You may think that you can do it without being hooked. But cigarettes are addictive, and they are one of the leading causes of death in the United States. If you don't want to start thinking about the long-term effects of smoking on your health, think about the effect on your wallet. One person figured out that he could have bought a Corvette with all the money he had spent on cigarettes!

These health issues should concern all youth. In addition, if you are sexually active, there are a number of other issues that you'll need to deal with.

CANCER

The incidence of cancer in teens is low. But sexual activity does increase the risk of certain forms of this disease.

Cancer of the testicles is the form most likely to be found in teenage males. If it is caught early, it is completely curable. Ask your doctor how to do a self-examination to detect early signs of this cancer, and get into the habit of doing this exam every month.

Teenage females should do monthly breast self-examinations. Although this form of cancer doesn't usually develop until later in life, early diagnosis is essential in its treatment.

Cancer of the cervix is another form that young women should be concerned with once they start having sex. Doctors can screen for cervical cancer with a test called a pap smear, which sexually active women should have once a year.

SEXUALLY TRANSMITTED DISEASES (STDs)

Though it may be a difficult issue to face, both personally and in discussions with your partner, anyone considering having sex must be aware that the world today is a sexually unsafe place. Every year, 2.5 to 3 million American teens contract one or more STDs. That does not include the hundreds of thousands infected each year with HIV, the virus that causes AIDS. No one is immune from these diseases. The myth that "nice" people don't get them is just that, a myth.

The only way you can reduce your risk of getting any of these diseases is by following safer sex guidelines. Note we said "safer" sex. Other than masturbation, there is no one-hundred-percent safe way to have sex. Safer sex is about decreasing the risk of contracting a disease, not eliminating it. The only way to eliminate that risk is abstinence. If you don't have sex, you won't get an STD. It's as simple as that.

If you are having sex, using a barrier (condoms, dental dams, latex gloves) is the safest form of protection. Barriers prevent the exchange of bodily fluids—blood, urine, stools, semen, and vaginal secretions—which can transmit disease. *Barriers do not remove all risk.* Condoms can break or slip off if not properly used, allowing bodily fluids to be exchanged. Gloves and dental dams can also develop small holes or tears, which are not always visible, through which germs can pass.

Some young people complain that stopping to get out a condom or barrier "kills the mood." Latex just isn't "romantic." Sure, latex may not have the same allure as candlelight and soft music. But nothing kills the mood faster than disease. And some STDs can kill you!

Condoms work best in preventing the germs of gonorrhea, syphilis, and chlamydia from being transmitted. They may not protect you against the transmission of genital warts or herpes, as the area of infection may extend beyond the area covered by the condom. Condoms should be worn during anal and oral sex, unrolled over the shaft of the penis when it is erect. The base of the condom should be held tight during withdrawal, so that the condom doesn't leak or slip off. Always use a water-based lubricant on the condom. *Don't* use a petroleum or oil-based product, such as Vaseline, massage oil, or baby oil. These will make the condom fall apart.

Lesbians take note: condoms can be your best friend, too. Dental dams, squares of latex which are stretched over a woman's genital area for protection during oral sex, are not as readily available as condoms; but a condom slit along one side and stretched out can serve the same purpose as a dam. Nonmicrowavable plastic wrap can also be used for protection during oral sex. If you're using a lubricant, make sure it's water based.

If you follow safer sex guidelines and use your own common sense, you can avoid STDs. In case you do contract one of these diseases, you also need to be aware of their symptoms and signs, which can often be mistaken for other illnesses.

Chlamydia

This is the most common STD. It does its damage silently, usually before any symptoms appear. It can be treated if caught in its early stages, which can be done by a screening test. If you have multiple partners, it's a good idea to get screened for this disease regularly.

Women are at particular risk from this disease because most will have no symptoms and not discover that they are infected until the disease has caused infertility by damaging the Fallopian tubes. A few infected women will experience some symptoms, which include burning urination, vaginal discharge, and pain in the pelvic area.

Men infected with chlamydia are more likely to have early symptoms than women; these include mild burning during urination and a penile discharge.

Genital Warts

In men, warts, which are caused by some strains of the human papilloma virus (HPV), usually appear as small bumps around the rectum. They can also appear on the penis. Women may have a more difficult time spotting these bumps inside the vagina. The warts are not painful, but they have been linked to the development of cancer of the penis, vulva, and cervix. There is no cure for the virus, but the warts can be removed by your doctor. However, the virus may remain after the warts have been removed, and they can reappear. The risk of infection is greatest when the warts are visible.

Genital Herpes

Painful lesions in the genital area that look like cold sores, sometimes accompanied by discharge from the penis or vagina, mark an outbreak of herpes. There is no cure for this viral infection, though the symptoms can be easily treated with drugs and salves. Attacks can come and go, and the virus can be dormant for years. As with genital warts, the chance of infection is greatest during one of these attacks, though there is also a risk when the sores are not in evidence.

Gonorrhea

This is frequently present at the same time as chlamydia, and can have the same long-term effect on women, damaging the Fallopian tubes and causing infertility. In women, the symptoms—a mild burning pain during urination, vaginal discharge, and/or light bleeding between menstrual periods—often go unnoticed or simply do not appear. Men are more likely to experience symptoms: pain or burning during urination, genital burning or itching, abdominal pain, and/or a cloudy-colored penile discharge. This disease is easily treated with antibiotics.

Hepatitis B

The symptoms of this disease are similar to those you get with the flu. Jaundice, a yellow discoloring of the skin, is another symptom. Hepatitis B is not strictly an STD; there are also other ways it can be transmitted. There are treatments to ease the symptoms, but the disease will eventually run its course and go away. A vaccine against this disease is available.

Syphilis

Genital lesions and lesions on the mouth, rectum, and nipples are the first symptoms of syphilis. Untreated, the sores will go away, though other symptoms—fever, aches, a rash, and/or a sore throat—will follow. If still untreated, the disease attacks the major body organs and it can be fatal. Syphilis must be treated early with antibiotics to prevent the disease from advancing through the body.

If you're not ready to talk about these issues with your partner, you're not ready to have sex. Your body may be ready. It may be telling your mind that it's raring to go! But you need to be emotionally and mentally ready, too. Being nervous or hesitant about discussing these issues is natural. Ignoring them is simply unacceptable. If you don't care about your own health, think about your partner's.

AIDS

If the facts about STDs don't convince you of the importance of following safer sex guidelines, consider this: AIDS is now the leading cause of death of young adults (people between the ages of 24 and 44) in America. If you have HIV, the virus that causes AIDS, and take good care of yourself, the virus is dormant for an average of 10.5 years before any symptoms of AIDS appear. During that time, you may not know you have HIV, and can be passing the virus to others every time you have unprotected sex.

AIDS is *not* a gay disease. It affects everyone. Today heterosexual transmission is the leading route of transmission. People who abuse intravenous drugs and share needles are one of the groups with the fastest growing rates of infection. Women are another. So are young people, regardless of sexual orientation.

AIDS can only be transmitted by the direct exchange of bodily fluids. The concentration of HIV is highest in blood and semen, lower in vaginal secretions. The virus is passed more readily from men to men and men to women than from women to men. Woman-to-woman transmission is the least likely. We know of a handful of cases, though unfortunately, little research has been done about lesbians and AIDS. Until more is known and until a cure is found, you must do all you can to protect yourself from this deadly virus. Educate yourself about HIV and AIDS. Use condoms or other latex barriers. Get tested for the HIV virus. Become a responsible adult—not a statistic.

SUBSTANCE ABUSE AND
HIGH-RISK BEHAVIOR

You don't need a doctor to tell you that being a teenager can be a tough and stressful experience. Balancing the pressures of school, family, work, and social life, determining who you are, and balancing what you need with what others expect of you is hard enough. Trying to do all this while coming to terms with the possibility of being gay may at times seem impossible. The need to find an escape from the stress and pressure can be overwhelming. That is why lesbians, gays, and bisexuals are at greater risk for drug and alcohol addiction than heterosexuals.

Here are the facts: according to a study by Dr. Emery Hetrick and Dr. A. Damien Martin, 80 percent of lesbian, gay, and bisexual youth report severe feelings of isolation. They feel that there's no one to talk to, that the distance is growing between themselves and their friends and family. They don't have the information they need to combat these feelings. This leads to the feeling that their lives have become meaningless. So why not take life to the edge? They start living dangerously, having unsafe sex, taking crazy risks, driving recklessly with no thought for their own safety or the safety of others. Many turn to drugs and alcohol to deal with their stress, anxiety, and depression. And many become alcoholics and drug addicts. Such addictions are not only bad for your physical health, but greatly increase your risk of injury and death due to accidents. And accidents are the leading cause of death for people under age 25.

As we said before, you don't have to feel isolated. You are not alone. There are places you can go and people you can turn to for help in dealing with your questions and concerns about your sexuality. There are also organizations that will help you deal with drug and alcohol problems. Both Alcoholics Anonymous and Narcotics Anonymous are open to gay teens, and many youth agencies have programs specifically for gays. Your doctor can also help. Your mental well-being is an integral part of your physical well-being. Doctors are pledged to protect both.

SUICIDE

Just as lesbian, gay, and bisexual youth are at greater risk for alcohol and drug addiction, they are at greater risk for suicide. The United States Department of Health and Human Services's 1989 *Report of the Secretary's Task Force on Youth Suicide* (which is being updated as of this writing) revealed that gay youth are two to three times more likely to attempt suicide than heterosexual youth. The report also estimated that up to 30 percent of the completed youth suicides every year are committed by lesbians, gays, and bisexuals—almost one in three suicides—though gays are only one in ten in the general population. Gays are also more likely to make multiple suicide attempts.

Suicidal feelings should *never* be taken lightly. If you feel life isn't worth living, that you can't cope with the pressure, get help! Talk to a trusted family member or friend; contact a doctor, a therapist, or a suicide hotline. You are a valuable member of society, a person with a lot to give and a lot to live for. If you've lost that knowledge, please contact someone who can help you find it again.

BISEXUAL HEALTH ISSUES

While bisexuals may face many of the same issues as lesbians and gays, they can also find themselves in a double bind: not being accepted in either the heterosexual or homosexual communities. Unfortunately, even lesbians and gays sometimes buy into the myth that bisexuals "just can't make up their minds." If you are attracted to both men and women and are having a hard time finding acceptance among friends and community, there are special support groups just for bisexuals.

In addition, bisexuals need to be aware of the signs and effects of STDs for both men and women. And of course, if you're having heterosexual sex, *use birth control*. If you are lesbian or gay and experimenting with heterosexual sex, don't think you can do without birth control, either.

Being lesbian or gay has nothing to do with your ability to conceive a child!

FINDING A DOCTOR OR
HEALTH-CARE PROVIDER

An essential part of maintaining good health is finding a doctor you trust and feel comfortable with. Maybe the person you usually see is also your family doctor, and you're nervous about opening up to her or him with questions about your sexuality. Sometimes this nervousness is justified. Unfortunately, not all doctors are gay-friendly.

If you're not sure where your doctor stands on homosexuality, you can try out a few simple questions, such as questions about AIDS and other sexually transmitted diseases, something many gay *and* straight youth are concerned about. Further questions might be "I'm having some concerns about my sexuality" or "How does sexual orientation happen?" Listen carefully to the doctor's responses—they'll give you clues as to where she or he stands on gay issues. If you then feel you're ready to jump in, you could try, "I wonder if I might be gay." You can always try the old "I have this friend who is worried about being gay. . . ." though that one's pretty easy to see through. You can also just look around the doctor's office for clues, such as gay-friendly or anti-gay posters and pamphlets on display.

You don't have to come out to your doctor—unless your sexuality is a factor in the condition you're being treated for. One set of symptoms might indicate the possibility of various different diseases, some of which are more common in gays than straight people, others more common in straight people than gays. Your doctor needs to have as much information as possible in order to make a correct diagnosis.

All doctors are sworn to obey strict confidentiality rules that prevent them from revealing anything their patients have discussed with them—even to the patient's parents—without the patient's permission. The only exception to this is if the patient is in a life-threatening situation, such as having thoughts of suicide, or being physically or sexually abused. Doctors are legally required to help prevent injury, which may involve breaking confidentiality.

If you want to see a new doctor of your own choosing, but don't want to tell your parents about it, and you don't have insurance or a lot of money, you can go to a public clinic. These frequently offer discounts or a sliding scale based on your income—or the lack of it. Friends can help you with referrals, or you could try phone referral services that won't charge to help you find a doctor. Most lesbian and gay community centers also keep lists of gay or "gay-friendly" doctors. You don't have to see a doctor who is gay—there are thousands of straight doctors who will give you capable and sensitive care.

Of course, you could be lucky, and have an experience like the one reported to us by Dr. Bentley Smith who, with Dr. Mary Fairbanks, helped us prepare this chapter. He was just walking out the door after treating a patient, when the patient said, "And by the way . . ." After a lot of hemming and hawing, the patient finally told him that he had previously had problems with other doctors because of his sexual orientation, and asked, "Do you mind that I'm gay?" Dr. Smith responded, "Do you mind that I am?" Thus was a wonderful doctor-patient relationship established.

CHAPTER SEVEN

MYTHS AND STEREOTYPES, AND HOW TO FIGHT THEM

"I love wearing Birkenstocks because they are comfortable, not because they define my sexual orientation. You won't find me on a Harley; does that means I'm not a true dyke?" —Ann, 16

"I was called a tomboy in elementary school because I played ball on the playground with the boys. This was very painful because I knew that they were using this word to hurt me."

—Leah, 17

Everyone knows how to recognize a homosexual, right? All gay men wear earrings, muscle T-shirts, cut-off jeans, and studded leather jackets, and have perfect hair. All lesbians wear flannel shirts, Doc Martens or

Birkenstock sandals, studded leather jackets, and no bras. But looks aren't the only way to tell. All gay men listen to disco—or opera—or Judy Garland, too. All lesbians listen to folk music—when they're not at a k.d. lang or Melissa Etheridge concert. We've also heard that:

▲ All lesbians play softball
◀ All gay men hate sports
▶ All lesbians have cats
▼ All gay men have small dogs
▲ All lesbians hate men
◀ All gay men hate women
▶ All lesbians want to be men
▼ All gay men want to be women
▲ All bisexuals are unable to make up their minds what they want to be
◀ All gay men are hairdressers or interior decorators
▶ All lesbians run food co-ops or feminist bookstores
▼ All homosexuals get along with each other—and they're all Democrats

Confused? So are the people who came up with these myths! And so would all gay people be if they had to live by them. What would you do if you were a lesbian and were allergic to cats? Or if you were a gay man who couldn't find that disco beat? Or if you were homosexual or bisexual and a Republican!

Relax. There is no such thing as gay hair, or lesbian shoes, or queer jobs. However, the pervasiveness of many of these myths and stereotypes is nothing to joke about.

What keeps myths and stereotypes alive? Rumor, gossip, and misinformation all contribute, but the biggest causes are ignorance and fear. And these are mutually perpetuating factors, each feeding on the other. Homophobic people—people with an irrational fear of homosexuality—use the myths to create "reasons" for their irrational fears, in the false belief that they can easily identify a homosexual. They believe that queers are "them" and readily distinguished from "us." Many claim not to know any homosexuals. When you consider that an estimated twenty-five million gay people live in the United States (based on the much-quoted statistic that one in ten people in this country is lesbian, gay, or bisexual), the odds on that claim being true are pretty slim. They may not know any "out" gay people, but they have met gay people out there, in their community, on the bus they take to work, in their schools and health clubs, and among their friends and aquaintances.

Of course, homophobes don't want to appear afraid of "them." And they don't want to be alone in their fear. So homophobes use the myths and stereotypes of homosexuality against the people they don't understand, to turn gays into the evil ones, and to make other people as afraid as they are. Myths and stereotypes then become the seeds of hate. Where they are sown, prejudice, discrimination, and violence frequently grow.

But being gay is not about the way the external world sees you, but how you see yourself. Most of the myths and stereotypes we listed at the beginning of this chapter concern appearances: those supposed "dead giveaway" clothes and behaviors. They say nothing about who you are as a person, about your values, morals, and beliefs. Being gay is about embracing your individuality and understanding your humanity—the things that make you "you"—not about living up (or down) to someone else's misconceptions.

In a perfect world everyone would get to know at least one lesbian, gay, or bisexual person. Everyone would come to understand that person, and understand that sexuality is only one facet of his or her personality, just as with heterosexuals. But homophobia usually develops early, often during childhood. A child who doesn't even know what "fag" or "dyke" means knows from listening to older people that the words can be used to hurt someone. And as these people grow older, they may continue to learn from ignorant people to hate and fear gays. They may find more ways to hurt, wounding with words and wounding with fists. Gay people didn't create this homophobia, any more than African-Americans created racism or Jews created anti-Semitism. Nor should they blame themselves if they find themselves its targets. But gays are responsible for combating homophobia.

SURVIVING IN A HOMOPHOBIC WORLD

Debunk the Myths

There are many myths about homosexuals that aren't simply based on ignorance or misinformation. They exist in open denial of the facts, with the aim of spreading fear, hate, and violence.

Myth: Homosexuality is sick and unnatural.

Fact: There is no medical or psychiatric institute or agency that still supports this. In December 1994, the American Medical Association House of Delegates issued a report calling for "nonjudgmental recognition of sexual orientation" by physicians. The American Pyschiatric Association stopped considering homosexuality a disorder in 1973, stating that, "It is no more abnormal or sick to be homosexual than to be left-handed."

Myth: Homosexuals are child molesters.

Fact: Studies show that child molesters are far more likely to be disturbed heterosexuals. Most sexual abuse of children takes place in a family setting, and is most often committed by a father or uncle against a female child. Outside the family, this abuse is committed primarily by pedophiles (people with a sexual perversion that makes them use children as sexual objects and has nothing to do with whether or not they are gay). Pedophiles are motivated more by hostility or the desire for power and control than by sexual desire—and, according to studies done in 1991 and 1994, 95 percent of pedophiles are male heterosexuals, and they victimize girls twice as often as boys.

Myth: Homosexuals recruit.

Fact: "Recruiting" is impossible. There is no social or scientific evidence that anyone can change your sexual orientation. In fact, if recruiting were possible, everyone would probably be heterosexual, given the pressure from the media, religious institutions, family, and society to be straight.

Myth: Homosexuals and bisexuals choose to be this way.

Fact: Sexual orientation is determined from infancy, if not biologically even before birth. Claims that homosexuals have been "cured" of their "choice" have all been proven to be hoaxes. The report of the AMA conference mentioned on the previous page also stated that they disapproved of "any attempt to change sexual orientation."

Use your common sense: would anyone *choose* to be in a minority that is the target of bigotry, hatred, and violence?

Myth: Homosexuals and bisexuals are unfit teachers.

Fact: Back in 1974, the nation's largest organization of public school teachers and employees, the National Education Association, added "sexual orientation" to its list of nondiscriminatory policies. We know that *no one* can change a person's sexual orientation and that a homosexual teacher is no more likely to molest students or try to "recruit" them than a heterosexual one. The Supreme Court of California agreed, ruling in 1969 in Morrison v. State Board of Education that a teacher's homosexuality alone was not cause enough to declare him "unfit to teach." However, the subject continues to be debated in other state courts.

Know the Law

Sticks and stones can break our bones, and name-calling is illegal! Name-calling is harassment regardless of who does it, and it is considered a hate crime by the federal government. In 1990, the federal government passed the National Hate Crime Statistics Act, which requires police departments around the country to report incidents of hate crimes motivated by prejudice—including those based on sexual orientation—to the Federal Bureau of Investigation (FBI). The police are then required to investigate the harassment to find out if indeed it was a hate crime, another type of offense, or a combination of the two, and also report these findings. How the hate crime is punished, however, is left up to each individual state's legislature.

You have the right to report incidents of name-calling, gay bashing, and violence based on sexual orientation. When you report harassment to a teacher, principal, victims' assistance center, anti-violence project, parent, or other adult, it is their responsibility to encourage you to report it to the police, or they can report it for you.

Know Your School's Policy on Harassment

Many schools—particularly those in the bigger cities of this country—are becoming more tolerant and respectful of their gay students. But even these schools aren't hanging out a welcome sign. As of this writing, Massachusetts is the only state with a law to protect lesbian, gay, and bisexual students from harassment. In all other states, students must rely on the protection provided by their individual school districts.

Every school district in the country has a policy about student conduct. This includes harassment. Some schools are now adding sexual orientation to the list of forms of harassment covered by their policy in order to protect lesbian, gay, and bisexual students from abuse by fellow students and staff.

Prepare for the Worst, Work Toward the Best

"In class one day, my teacher said that all fags are child molesters and should be shot. I took him aside after class and told him that I didn't approve of his comments because my brother is gay. I told him that if he didn't stop I would report him to the principal. The next day he apologized to the class and said that his comments the day before were inappropriate and that he expects the class to respect all people," says Tina, 18.

This is how one young woman chose to deal with a homophobic comment. How would you have handled the situation in Tina's classroom?

Harassment is frequently an unpleasant reality. How you deal with it is critically important. You need to have a plan. You need to know when to shrug it off and when to do something about it. If you decide to act, there is a lot you have to consider: Is the situation dangerous? How can I get away safely? Who can I tell? Who will believe me? Will fighting back or telling someone make the situation worse?

We received many reports of serious harassment from gay students around the country. Students were singled out by teachers for verbal abuse. One student was thrown against her locker by a basketball player who called her a "dyke." Entire groups of students called out "fag" or "dyke" at gay students during every passing period. The stories varied, but they all had two things in common. Students were hurt. And they were scared.

One common situation which many students identified was harassment by a gang. In one story typical of this situation, a group of macho high-school boys formed a gang. Their goal was to make life at their school so difficult for lesbian, gay, and bisexual students that they would be forced to leave. The gang started out with name-calling, but their activities soon escalated to pushing, hitting, and threatening serious violence.

Six students in different parts of the country faced gangs such as this. Here's how they dealt with the harrassment:

▼ Maria asked her friend, a football player, to walk her past the gang to her classroom. The gang didn't want to risk dealing with the football player, and they finally let Maria alone.

▼ Peter, on the other hand, felt sure enough of himself to simply ignore the taunts and threats. Despite several weeks of harassment, Peter refused to let it get to him, and the gang eventually gave up their taunts.

▼ Jackie believed she should fight back and returned the name-calling. But the attack escalated when the gang cornered her and pummeled her until a teacher intervened. The members of the gang were suspended. However, teachers could not stop the verbal harrassment when the gang returned to school.

▼ Bill talked to his counselor, who consulted with the local lesbian and gay anti-violence project (AVP). In turn, the AVP was asked to conduct a hate-crime workshop for all students and staff. Attendance was mandatory, which made the workshop a success and ended the gang harassment.

▼ Mel, experiencing a sudden adrenaline rush, pushed one of the gang members into a locker, retaliating for months of harassment. The level of abuse from her fellow classmates dropped off and she graduated safely.

▼ Jenny turned immediately to the school counselor and the principal. When they would not help, Jenny and her parents hired an attorney and sued her school district for not protecting her right to a safe and equitable education.

Even given the same basic situation, you can't count on any one response being effective. You have to be aware of all the options. Every situation of verbal and physical harassment or abuse is different. There may be a problem at your school where a person in authority—a teacher, principal, or student counselor—cannot or will not take measures to protect you, or is even the cause of the problem. In that case, you must find someone who will listen and act on your behalf. You may have to change classes to avoid a particular teacher who makes anti-gay comments. Some students have gone so far as to change schools. Laura, 16, even changed school districts, moving in with her aunt to complete her high-school education.

If you're lucky, you'll graduate from school without ever having to face any difficulties. But if you are faced with harassment, in or out of school, here are some ways to deal with it:

▼ Take a self-defense course. This can not only teach you how to protect yourself but give you physical and mental confidence at a time when your confidence is being shaken.

▼ Find someone who will be supportive. A friend, relative, or counselor can help you deal with the emotional pain of harassment, and might help you deal with the harassment itself.

▼ Ask your parents or another adult to help you file a complaint.

▼ Call a local lesbian and gay community center for advice on dealing with the situation. They can refer you to an advocate or caseworker who will help you come up with the best solution—and they are completely confidential.

▼ If you want to bring legal action against a harasser, you can get help in finding an attorney in your area from the American Civil Liberties Union (ACLU), the Lambda Legal Defense Fund, or your local gay and lesbian community center.

▼ Report all hate crimes to the National Gay and Lesbian Task Force, who help the FBI and local authorities keep track of hate-crime statistics, or to one of the anti-violence projects, which are listed in the Resources section at the back of the book. The AVP will give you sound advice and can offer direct help, regardless of where you live.

Other possibilities if you are being harassed in school:

▼ Report the harassment to a teacher or other faculty member. Make sure you can trust this person. He or she must be able to act on your behalf.

▼ Report the harassment to your principal. If your principal won't do anything about the situation, make an appointment to meet with the superintendent of schools.

▼ Ask your principal to arrange special classes in conflict resolution. In these classes, teachers and students will learn strategies for the peaceful settling of differences.

▼ Change classes or schools if serious harassment continues.

▼ Above all else: get your education! This is your right. Don't let anyone take it away from you.

Being yourself in a world that encourages conformity isn't easy. You have to decide what's comfortable for you—and what's safe. Maybe you want to dress like the popular students, to blend in with the crowd. Or maybe you want to be as out as possible, declaring who you are with a NOBODY KNOWS I'M GAY T-shirt. There is no right or wrong appearance, no stereotype you have to fit. But there are right and wrong actions, and a range of options you can follow if you feel you've been wronged. All gays and straights have an equal right to a safe and equitable education. If someone is preventing you from exercising that right, it's your right to do something about it.

Chapter Eight

Keeping the Faith:
Religion and Spirituality

"Nothing can replace church; only my sexuality makes it impossible to go. I don't pray, I don't meditate and I don't read the Bible anymore."

—Lynn, 16

"Look, I don't always worry about the future. But I worry about today. Deep down in my heart, I want to be able to go to church—to know that God still loves me. After all, God loved me before I came out. Why can't He love me today?"   —Kevin, 17

Of all the subjects we raised in our interviews for this book, the one which elicited the saddest responses and revealed the most frustration and anxiety among our young respondents was the subject of religion and spirituality.

Many young people seem to have lost their faith and run away from any involvement with their religious institutions upon discovering their homosexuality. They believe that by accepting their homosexuality they ceased to be acceptable to their church or synagogue. Not only is this sad, and in some cases tragic, it's also not true.

Most of this country's religious institutions display deeply ambivalent feelings about gay issues. In many cases, these ambivalences are the source of great controversy among church leaders and within their congregations. The Roman Catholic church, for example, is currently embroiled in divisive debate over homosexuality. In 1992, the Vatican issued a statement outlining the church's position that homosexuality is an "objective disorder." Catholics should in effect, "love the sinner, but hate the sin." The Vatican statement also said that Catholic bishops should oppose homosexual anti-discrimination legislation in the areas of adoption, child placement, military service, or employment of teachers and athletic coaches, and oppose sex education or any AIDS prevention eduction that mentions condoms. However, individual congregations and church members have stood against their leaders on many of these issues. In fact, one of the largest religious organization for gays and lesbians, Dignity, was founded by members of the Roman Catholic church—although the group is not recognized by the Vatican.

While many religious communities and institutions are debating their church's policies on homosexuality, some religious organizations are taking the debate into the larger community. Today, the most vocal group denouncing homosexuals is the radical Christian right, a group of people from a variety of churches with a biblical literalist tradition and a political agenda of seeing their beliefs enforced by government. Biblical literalists believe that all evil in the world can be overcome by reading the Bible and following it word for word in the most literal sense, as if it were a legal document. The radical Christian right can quote chapter and verse from the Bible to justify their beliefs about how life should be lived not just by members of their churches but by everyone. They believe simply that homosexuality is an abomination, that all homosexuals are damned, and that all homosexuals are a threat to "traditional" American families. They base their beliefs on their interpretation of a handful of biblical passages, texts which other religious institutions also use in their debates on homosexuality. So let's go right to the source of the controversy.

One of the passages in the Old Testament that is most often cited as a condemnation of homosexuality is Leviticus 18:22, which says, "You shall not lie with a male as with a woman; it is an abomination." A few verses later, Leviticus 20:13 adds the penalty: "If a man lies with a male as with a woman, both of them have committed an abomination; they shall be put to death, their blood is upon them." For biblical literalists, there's no way to argue with that. But if you do take this injunction literally, wouldn't you need to take every other command in the Bible equally literally? There also is a passage in the Old Testament that prescribes the death penalty for people who loan money at interest (Ezekiel 18:5–18). Should bankers be cast out of the flock? Should they even be allowed to live? And what about the many practices the Old Testament condones that are not acceptable today, such as slavery, animal sacrifice, polygamy, and treating women as property? Should these practices be allowed according to the teachings given by the Bible?

Obviously, biblical literalists are selective in what biblical laws they choose to follow. It is simply not possible to live in modern times in the same way that people lived thousands of years ago. As the Reverend Elder Dr. Charles Arehart of the Metropolitan Community Church of the Rockies states, "Religious belief has always had a historical relationship to a particular time and culture."

We should consider the laws of Leviticus in terms of the time when they were first applied. The Israelites were then a scattered group of tribes. They were traveling in search of a homeland, surrounded by hostile peoples against whom they had to defend themselves and their religious beliefs. Because their numbers were so few, God's injunction to "be fruitful and multiply" had to be taken very seriously. In numbers they would find strength; it was a matter of simple survival. The Israelites also believed that men were solely responsible for procreation, that sperm contained all the elements of life; women were merely the "vessel" in which the seed grew. So "spilling the seed," through masturbation or nonreproductive sex, was a grave sin. It was also important for the Israelites to separate themselves from the more widely followed pagan religions of the times, some of which incorporated homosexual rituals in their fertility rites. Participating in male homosexual acts (the Bible never directly mentions female homosexuality) wasn't just against Israelite law, it was also seen as a rejection of their small, struggling community. Given our current understanding of human reproduction, the probable genetic basis of homosexuality, and the fact that overpopulation is far more of a threat today than underpopulation, homosexuality can no longer be perceived as a threat to or a rejection of the community.

The other most widely cited biblical condemnation is the story of Sodom and Gomorrah, which first appears in Genesis (18:16–19:29). When two male angels travel to Sodom to try to find ten righteous people and so prevent the city's destruction by God, they spend the night as Lot's guests. A mob gathers demanding to "know" the angels, that is to rape them. So as not to violate the laws of hospitality, Lot instead offers the mob his two virgin daughters to do with as they please. The Christian radical right says that the mob's homosexual desire is "the sin of Sodom"—leaving out that their intent was rape. Yet when the story of Sodom is told elsewhere in the Old Testament, other explanations of Sodom's sin are given. In Ezekiel 16:49, Ezekiel says, "Behold, this was the guilt of your sister Sodom: she and her daughters had pride, surfeit of food, and prosperous ease, but did not aid the poor and needy." In the books of Isaiah and Jeremiah, the sins of Sodom are described as arrogance, adultery, insincere religious practices, political corruption, oppression of the poor, and neglect of the fatherless and the widowed. The term *sodomy* for the sexual act between men is nowhere used in the Bible; it was first invented by biblical scholars in the first century A.D.

In the New Testament, Jesus in Luke 10:10–13 speaks of inhospitality to the messengers of God as the sin that will bring down God's vengeance as it was brought down on Sodom. And what does Jesus say about homosexuality? Absolutely nothing. Jesus welcomed all people and made love and compassion the basis for his discipleship: "A new commandment I give to you, that you love one another; even as I have loved you. . . . By this all men will know that you are my disciples, if you have love for one another" (John 13:34–35).

In the New Testament, it is the teachings of St. Paul, particularly in Romans 1:26–27 and 1 Corinthians

6:9–11, that are most often cited against homosexuality. In both passages, however, there is some debate about whether the Greek words in the original text can even be translated as "homosexual" (they are not done so in either the King James version or the Revised Standard version). Many scholars believe that the words used in Corinthians refer to the idolatrous practice of temple prostitution, not to homosexuality at all. And in the passage from Romans, Paul regards "homosexuality" as a punishment accorded to idolaters and those who were unfaithful to God—it is not the sin but its consequence. Paul may also have foreseen that this passage could be used to unfairly condemn others, as he followed it with, "You have no excuse, O man, whoever you are, when you judge another; for in passing judgement upon him you condemn yourself" (Romans 2:1).

The teachings of Paul should also be understood in the light of his belief that Jesus was returning—not in millennia, but any day. Procreation was no longer necessary; preparing for the Lord's imminent return was his priority. Dr. Charles Arehart comments, "To put it simply, Paul believed that if you put your earthly interests above your spiritual relationship with God, then you are tempted away from God. Paul even believed it was better not to marry; his distant second choice was to marry if you can't control yourself."

It is always necessary for you—for all people—to

remember that the writers of and the commentators on the Bible were, first of all, mere human beings, and secondly, almost exclusively men. They are, as all humans are, fallible and subject to the misinformation and emotional and prejudicial attitudes of their own time and culture. "Who today would share Paul's anti-Semitic attitude, his belief that the authority of the state was not to be challenged or that all women ought to be veiled?" asks Bishop John S. Spong of the Episcopal Diocese of Newark, New Jersey.

In various historical times, the Bible has been used to foster peace—but also, unfortunately, persecution. It was the most devout Catholics who ordered the expulsion, torture, and burning of Jews, homosexuals, and heretics during the Spanish Inquisition, justifying their actions by the Bible. Many people in the past have claimed righteousness as the basis for unrighteous actions, in direct opposition to the Judeo-Christian tradition, and regrettably, many still do. But the Bible is not theirs alone to interpret. The Bible is above all else a testament to love: God's all-inclusive love for each of us, our love for God and for each other.

Many different religions have organizations for gay members. You'll find a full listing of these groups in the Resources section at the back of this book. But if you are in a church or synagogue that treats you with hostility, that denies your existence or asks that you lead your life as a lie, that promotes harassment, homophobia, and hatred amongst its members, it may not be worth keeping it in your life. As the Reverend Elder Dr. Arehart says, "It hurts your relationship with God to be constantly at war with yourself. And being at war with yourself means living a life of pretense, not being true to yourself, keeping part of yourself hidden from God."

Jesse, 17, says, "I seem to have lost whatever spirituality I once had when I left my religion, as if I also left behind everything I had learned in church all the years I attended with my family." Even if, after recognizing your sexuality, you feel you cannot attend your family church, you don't have to lose your spirituality. "Spirituality," says Rabbi Susan Freeman of Congregation B'nai Israel in Northampton, Massachusetts, "is a way of doing and being that connects you to something greater. It is those moments of connection that elevate you from the mundane to the more meaningful. It is a way of life that prescribes a personal moral and ethical relationship to God."

Rabbi Freeman, like other thoughtful, concerned leaders of many religious faiths, believes that whether you are a Buddhist, Christian, Jew, Catholic, or member of any other religion, you can find an accepting religious community.

"The great message of Scripture is of a God of unbounded love for the human family," says Bishop Stanley

E. Olson, retired pastor and bishop of the Evangelical Lutheran Church in America. And this love is unqualified, freely given to all God's children.

As long as you maintain your ability to question, to search for your own answers, and to believe, you will be able to find a spiritual community that will welcome you. Accepting yourself as a sexual being does not mean surrendering your life as a spiritual being. The sense of belonging, of support, and of community that religious groups may provide can be an invaluable help to you in your journey toward self-acceptance. It's important not to let the inhumane words and actions of a few keep you from fully exercising and exploring your own spirituality.

CHAPTER NINE

WHERE WE'VE BEEN AND WHERE WE'RE GOING

"Gay history is one of the things that keeps our community alive." —*Andie, 17*

History isn't just dates, names, and places to be memorized. History helps us to know our place in the world, to discover where we're going by tracing where we've been. People of all ethnic, religious, and political heritages can take pride in the historical accomplishments of their people. Gay people also share a sense of historical pride in their own heritage and can find inspiration in the lives of gay heros. You can take comfort from the historical fact that you are not now, and have never been, alone. The tradition and continuity of gay history can strengthen you and give you a sense of community on your individual journey toward self-acceptance. After all, gay pride grows in part from the seeds of gay history.

Many scientists, sociologists, and historians believe that homosexuality has existed as long as humans have. The contemporary understanding of homosexuality, however, is different in many ways from that of past eras. Our society's evolution has limited classification of a person's sexual identity to just three categories: gay, straight, or bisexual. These labels don't always fit the bill. Other modern cultures do exist with less rigid definitions of sexual orientations. Many Native American cultures, for example, have no categories of sexuality at all. They value a range of sexual orientations, in the belief that this reveals a wider spiritual connection to male and female spirits.

In the West, gay culture can be traced back at least as far as the classical Greek and Roman worlds that provided us with the model for our democratic government and the roots of our language. We can also look to these civilizations for examples of tolerance and acceptance of homosexuality.

Though the word *lesbian* (from Lesbos, the island where the lesbian poet Sappho lived) comes from the ancient Greek, less is known about female homosexuality than male homosexuality in ancient history. All we know about Sappho is that she was probably married and had a daughter, and, most important, that she wrote beautiful love poems addressed both to men and to women. Women had a very low status in Greco-Roman civilizations and were generally confined to their homes and forbidden to participate in public affairs. During most of the following periods, women's lives were still not considered a fitting subject for the history of *man*kind, so there is little historical information available on lesbians. Therefore, most of our pre–twentieth century historical overview will only be able to deal with male homosexuality.

In ancient Greece, it was common practice for an aristrocratic young man or boy to be "apprenticed" to an older man, who would act as his teacher and role model, training him in the ways of politics, culture, warfare, and love. It was not unacceptable for the older man to have a sexual relationship with his charge. Today such relations between a man and a boy are illegal and considered a serious form of abuse, harmful to a boy's sense of self and well-being. In ancient Greece, however, this apprentice relationship was considered a natural part of education and growing up. Young men were also expected to marry later and raise a family, but continued relationships with men were not generally frowned upon.

This type of bisexuality was expected and accepted in ancient Greek culture, at least for men. We know that Greek men did have sexual and love relationships with other men without any sense of guilt or shame or fear of community disapproval.

The ancient Greeks even had what could be thought of as "gay events." The first Olympic games were virtually male beauty pageants, with athletes competing in the nude before an all-male audience. Homosexuality in the military wasn't only accepted, it was encouraged. It was believed that a soldier fighting alongside his lover would fight more courageously, both to protect his loved one and so that he would not appear cowardly in his lover's eyes. Some of the great war heroes of Greek history and legend, such as Alexander the Great and Achilles, were known to have adult male lovers.

The Romans didn't have institutionalized models of homosexuality as the Greeks did. Still, the practice was common and generally tolerated. Take the story of the Egyptian Queen Cleopatra's love affairs with Mark Antony and Julius Caesar, for example. These heterosexual affairs were considered far more scandalous at the time than either man's previous homosexual relationships. It is widely believed that Julius Caesar was the young lover of King Nicomedes of Bithnynia. Despite some disapproval of this relationship from conservative Romans, Caesar rose to expand Rome's far-flung empire and become its ruler. Caesar's friend and rival Mark Antony also took male lovers as a young man. In fact, his enemies claimed he was little better than a male prostitute. But these affairs did not cause either man any real trouble. That came from their relations with a foreign woman and powerful ruler, Cleopatra.

Little historical evidence is available about homosexuality in the millennium following the downfall of the Roman Empire, during the main period of growth of the Catholic church. Opinions vary widely on the subject, although historian John Boswell in his book *Christianity, Social Tolerance and Homosexuality* has made a compelling argument for the existence of a thriving gay culture and general tolerance of homosexuality until roughly A.D. 1150. There is ample documentation, however, of the wave of church- and government-ordained homosexual persecution that followed.

In 1307, King Philip of France launched an attack against the Knights Templar, a brotherhood of military monks that had existed for over two hundred years. Knights were accused of witchcraft and homosexuality, tortured until they confessed, and burned at the stake. The brotherhood was destroyed—and its vast riches went to the king, which was probably his real motivation for the persecution. Similar church-ordered homosexual witch-hunts took place in fifteenth-century Spain during the infamous Spanish Inquisition. Some scholars believe that the modern slang word for a homosexual male, *faggot*, which literally means a bundle of sticks, comes from this time period because homosexuals were burned to death like kindling for a fire. How much of this persecution was due to intolerance of homosexuality and how much was due to the religious and political upheavals of the times is a subject of debate.

The five hundred years from the 1400s to the 1900s saw periods both of tolerance and of persecution of homosexuals. Records of trials by both religious and social authorities testify not only to the persecution of homosexuals, but also to the fact that lesbians, gays, and bisexuals were frequently living and working equitably alongside their heterosexual peers. Artists and authors of the Renaissance and Baroque eras also left behind in their artworks and writings evidence that they were free to explore homosexuality.

In this period, Western society as a whole was moving toward a standardized social structure in which sexuality was not spoken of. The lives of everyday people of the time were not preserved in literature or history. Not until the Industrial Revolution, when hordes of people—particularly young people—moved to the cities, did the masses and how they lived their lives become part of the historical record. But for the upper classes of Victorian society, sexuality was a taboo subject. The one obvious fact is that homosexuality is a historical reality, although the rejection of homosexuality has marked most of Western history. Views on homosexuality have always changed with the prevailing religious, political, and social status quo.

In our own century, the patchwork pattern of tolerance and persecution continues. Germany, for example, was the site of both the first modern movement for tolerance and acceptance of homosexuality and the worst slaughter of homosexuals. In 1919, Magnus Hirshfeld founded the Institute for Sex Research, which became internationally known and respected for its studies of all forms of human sexuality. Hirshfeld believed that homosexuality was a "deep inner-constituted natural instinct," a statement he first made in 1896. During the 1920s, major cities of Germany, Berlin in particular, had thriving gay cultures.

But all tolerance ceased in the years of Adolf Hitler's rise to power. Hitler and his Nazi party denounced homosexuality as a threat to the "moral purity" of the German nation, and began a relentless campaign of homosexual persecution. Thousands of European gay men were sent to the same concentration camps that saw the slaughter of six million Jews. No one knows how many gays died in the camps, but those who were still alive when the Allies liberated the camps were not immediately released. The Allies and the West German government the Allies put in power after World War II believed that gay men were criminals and a danger to the general population.

America in the 1920s and 1930s also saw the creation of a booming gay culture. Bohemian neighborhoods such as Harlem and Greenwich Village in New York provided cabarets, clubs, and private parties where lesbians, gays, and bisexuals met. It was an era of experimentation and tolerance where gays enjoyed a freedom they had not known for centuries before.

World War II brought further improvements for lesbians, and for women in general, in the United States. With the male workforce leaving to fight overseas, women were more or less drafted to take men's places in factories, plants, and offices. Many women also joined the military, where lesbian life thrived. Women could now earn their own salaries, run their own households, and even adopt the less constricting fashions previously limited to men: pants and short hair. In this atmosphere, it became easier for lesbians to meet, to come out, and to gain financial independence. The lesbian community grew in strength, numbers, and visibility.

The end of World War II and the beginning of the Cold War, however, signaled a new wave of homosexual repression in America. Senator Joseph McCarthy whipped Americans into a frenzy of anti-communist fear—and he lumped homosexuals, along with many other "un-American" people, in with the supposed communist conspiracy. Many gay lives were destroyed when people lost their jobs and their reputations under McCarthy's government-sponsored campaign to identify and punish supposed communists.

The 1950s also saw the beginnings of the movement for homosexual rights, with the work of the Mattachine Society and the Daughters of Bilitis, who put out newspapers and sponsored protests and demonstrations in favor of tolerance toward homosexuals. Then the "sexual revolution" of the 1960s and the women's liberation movement of the 1970s opened the way for a broader acceptance of homosexuals in America and a chance for gay culture and gay communities to grow and thrive.

The modern "gay liberation movement" officially began on June 27, 1969, at a bar called the Stonewall Inn in New York's Greenwich Village. For the first time, lesbians, gay men, bisexuals, drag queens, leather dykes, and students fought back against the police and their almost nightly raids of gay bars. The participants didn't know it at the time, but during the subsequent three nights of street fighting—called the Stonewall Riots—they were beginning the new gay civil rights crusade. There arose a new call for homosexuals to come out, organize, and fight for their basic civil rights.

A year after that first riot, five thousand women and men marched in New York to commemorate the Stonewall uprising and to send out a "call for action" to the homosexual and bisexual community. That was the first Gay Freedom or Gay Pride Day. In 1994, a quarter of a century after the Stonewall Riots, New York's Gay Pride weekend drew close to one million people, who joined in the marches, demonstrations, and festivities, and the week-long gay Olympics, Gay Games IV. The ancient Greeks never got such a turnout!

So where does history find us today?

In the two-and-a-half decades since the Stonewall Riots, the gay community has begun to develop and cherish a sense of historical tradition. They recognize the courage shown by past individuals and organizations fighting for homosexual rights and freedoms and are continuing to build on that tradition.

Politically, gay rights have been discussed and fought for—and against—with an openness and vigor unseen previously in this century. Of course, the cycle of progress and backlash continues. There have been countless attempts to pass laws on state and local levels specifically protecting gay civil rights, and there have been many efforts to deny them. In 1993, twelve states proposed restrictive constitutional amendments which could bar civil-rights protections for gays. In 1994, two states—Idaho and Oregon—defeated such legislation. The fate of Colorado's antigay initiative, Amendment 2, which passed, still hangs in the balance, awaiting a U.S. Supreme Court hearing.

What has been notable in all these political battles has been not merely the united action of the gay community, but the support from the wider community. People of all sexual orientations, faiths, and political beliefs joined forces to fight for not just gay rights but human rights. In Oregon, for example, while the radical Christian right led the campaign for the antigay Ballot Measure 9 in 1992, people of other religions formed People of Faith Against Bigotry. Their strong and united voice helped to defeat the measure.

The AIDS crisis, which has cost hundreds of thousands of lives, has also helped to galvanize the gay community into action, leading to the formation of such powerhouse organizations as the AIDS Coalition to Unleash Power (ACT UP) and the Gay Men's Health Crisis (GMHC). As the AIDS epidemic touches everyone, regardless of age, gender, faith, or sexual orientation, so has the fight against it brought together all types of people, gay and straight.

These battles are all ongoing, and you can make a difference in any of them, for history is made not just by organizations, but by individuals. Many lesbian, gay, and bisexual young people express the need for gay role models—past and present. Role models can provide a certain kind of support for an individual, a sense of relatedness and possibility. When visible and out lesbians, gays, and bisexuals empower others within the gay community, they also create an awareness of lesbian, gay, and bisexual issues in mainstream society. Perhaps most importantly, they can also reinforce the truth that you are not alone—even on days and nights when you are least able to believe it.

Significant contributions to history have been made by homosexuals whether or not their sexual orientation has been public. No doubt you've read about many individuals in your history books or in the newspapers without knowing their sexual orientation. And just as certainly, some of them were or are gay. Knowing who these people are can help battle stereotypes—other peoples' as well as the ones in your own thinking.

Look in the history books, on the pop charts, in newspapers and magazines, and you will find lesbians, gays, and bisexuals who have made and are making a difference. These people can make a difference in your life, too, whether you want to follow their examples and work for positive change, or just need to find a little inspiration to get you through the day. It has been said that "Those who do not know history are condemned to repeat it." The opposite is just as true. If you know history, know what progress has been made and what work there is still to do, you can be the movers and shakers, the makers of new history.

CHAPTER TEN

YOUTH IN THE LEAD

"This is the first generation of out youth who don't take abuse from society. Our leadership has to realize that the youth movement is a needed force behind the gay movement at large."

—Tim, 19

"The youth movement is like a quiet voice which is slowly reaching a loud scream." *—Joe, 19*

Historically, young people have been at the forefront of nearly every significant movement for political action that has taken place throughout the world. During the American civil rights movement of the 1960s, young people were frequently in the vanguard at sit-ins and protests, marching bravely with Martin Luther King, Jr., and his associates. The anti–Vietnam War movement of the late 1960s and early 1970s gained momentum from the young people who were also an integral part of its early beginnings. In China, students led the revolt against government oppression when they occupied Tiananmen Square.

These are only a few of the moments in history when young people, filled with idealism and courage, focused their energy and power to encourage debate and demand change from the old order. Young people were also active at the very beginning of the modern gay rights movement. After the Stonewall Riots of 1969, lesbian and gay students at Hunter College in New York were quick to form a student support group. Today, young people are moving to the forefront of the gay rights movement, both in established organizations and in a host of newly formed groups.

An increasing number of school districts and individual schools have developed programs and policies supporting gay youth, thanks in part to the work of Massachusetts Governor William Weld. The governor was appalled by the statistics on gay teen suicide in the United States Department of Health and Human Services's 1989 *Report of the Secretary's Task Force on Youth Suicide*. On February 10, 1992, he signed an executive order to create the first Governor's Commission on Gay and Lesbian Youth. This commission, made up of students, teachers, parents, and professionals, was formed to look into the issues facing lesbian, gay, and bisexual students in their schools. With testimony from these young people, their parents and others, the gay students' plight was finally revealed to the general public, the media, and policy makers. The commission found that the harassment and violence encountered by many lesbian, gay, and bisexual youth in schools interfered with their right to a safe and complete education. The governor then signed into law a safe schools policy that gave lesbian, gay, and bisexual young people protection in the schools, including due process in cases of harassment, access to information, and referrals to gay-related services and materials.

The two largest educators' organizations in the United States, the National Education Association and the American Federation of Teachers, have both issued policy statements calling for an end to harassment, and the establishment of support programs for gay students. In Massachusetts alone, over one hundred schools have student gay and gay/straight alliance organizations. More are forming all the time, particularly in the areas around major cities such as New York, Chicago, Miami, and Minneapolis. Still, the biggest change in schools has been that more and more lesbian, gay, and bisexual students are fighting for their own rights, working to change their fellow students' attitudes and their schools' policies.

Tony, 17, is his senior class president. Though he is not

out to any of his peers, he doesn't stand by while other students are abused. When he told a classmate not to call another classmate a "fag," the classmate stopped, out of respect for Tony.

Nicki, age 16, successfully lobbied the counseling department of her high school to add the local gay and lesbian community center's phone number to the students' hotline reference list.

Jen, 20, believes, "I can really make a difference by helping other people. Currently I'm serving on a youth board [of a lesbian, gay, and bisexual community center] and I'm a peer counselor."

In 1994, the students of Shawnee Mission High School stood together against school censorship. When members of their Kansas school district board tried to remove several "controversial" books—books with lesbian and gay themes—from the library shelves, the students acted quickly. They checked out three thousand books from their school library in one day! Chaos reigned, and the school board got the message: all students must have total access to all books. The so-called controversial books were all returned to the shelves.

In the past few years, young people have also begun leading the fight for their rights within gay political organizations. The National Gay and Lesbian Task Force (NGLTF) has long been a leader in lobbying and working for gay rights. At their 1993 "Creating Change" conference, young lesbians, gays, and bisexuals demanded that NGLTF creates a youth board seat on its board of directors and that they open up staff positions for youth in the divisions of NGLTF which work on youth issues. The young people got their board seat and staff membership.

Young people from around the country also organized the first Youth Empowerment Speakout (YES), which was held on April 24, 1993, during the March on Washington. The event attracted almost 600 women and men between the ages of fourteen and twenty-four, making it the largest speaking event ever organized by and for gay youth. The young people listened to speakers and joined discussion groups about the issues they faced, including teen suicide, violence against lesbian, gay, and bisexual students, and school harassment, which frequently leads students to drop out. The following day, 1,500 young people marched behind the YES banner, making themselves heard with chants such as, "Two, four, six, eight. Are you sure your kids are straight?!"

One of the sponsors of YES, a group leading in the creation of youth-run programs, is the National Advocacy Coalition on Youth and Sexual Orientation (NACYSO). NACYSO was founded in 1992 by Frances Kunreuther, Executive Director of the Hetrick-Martin Institute, which serves roughly 1,500 young people every year. Young members of NACYSO participate in all aspects of the organization, running committees, participating in political lobbying, and coordinating actions with "allies," non-gay mainstream agencies working to better the lives of all young people.

Young gay people today realize that the gay community cannot work alone for change, but must work hand in hand with other organizations concerned with basic human rights. They also realize that they are part of a larger community, not just part of the "gay community." Just as community groups concerned with women's rights, the rights of African-Americans, or environmental issues have contributed to the gay rights movement, young gay people can make contributions to these groups in turn.

All of these examples illustrate the various ways that young people are involved in making change on personal, interpersonal, community, state, and national levels. It doesn't matter whether you're out or not, your energy, your voice, and your ideas can make a difference. When you are ready, here are some suggestions about ways you can be involved:

▼ Educate your family, friends, and peers about respecting and tolerating all people regardless of their differences.

▼ Talk to and support your lesbian, gay, and bi-sexual peers.

▼ March in your local Gay Pride Parade or take part in other gay events such as sports competi-

tions, candlelight vigils, fundraisers, and con-
certs in the lesbian, gay, and bisexual communities.

▼ Support, encourage, and work toward the elim-
ination of injustice, harassment, and violence in
your home, school, and workplace.

▼ Find out what's happening in your state legislature and in Congress and let your representative
know how you feel. You'll find phone numbers
and addresses for your city, state, and federal
representatives in the United States Government
section of the telephone book.

▼ Write a letter to a teacher, administrator, local
newspaper, or television station if you are dis-
satisfied with how you or your lesbian, gay, and
bisexual peers are treated. You are entitled to an
equal education, in addition to information and
referrals. You are also entitled to your anony-
mity and confidentiality.

▼ Speak out on the issues facing lesbian, gay, and
bisexual young people. Many community centers have a speakers' bureau sponsored by groups
specific to gay youth.

▼ Organize against book banning at your school
or local library.

▼ Support your local gay-owned or gay-friendly
businesses and organizations.

▼ Volunteer for a group or community center where you can stuff envelopes, become a peer counselor, organize an event or fundraiser, and so on.

▼ Volunteer for other causes outside of the lesbian, gay, and bisexual community. Other community and national organizations have helped the gay community in many ways. They, too, need your help and support.

▼ Get involved with school activities and organizations.

▼ Get your education and don't stop learning! There is nothing more empowering than education.

For more information on how you can become involved, see the Resource section at the back of this book for an organization or group in your community. If there is no agency or organization near you, contact the national organizations also listed to find out how you can make a difference. The opportunities are there. All you have to do is take advantage of them.

EPILOGUE: THE BEST OF ALL POSSIBLE WORLDS

The issues in this book may seem theoretical to some people. But for the young people who have contributed their thoughts and their stories, they are very real—as real as the fears, sorrows, confusion, and poignant humor that their words express.

That these young people pay a price for their sexual orientation comes through loud and clear. This price can be lessened in many ways by parents, friends, teachers, counselors, and others. Through their understanding and caring, they can help young people get through the passage into adulthood and help them to lead happy and productive lives.

Since this is a book for, about, and in some ways, by gay teens—it couldn't have been written without them—

it is only fitting that they should have the final word. In the interviews we held and the questionnaires we distributed, we asked what would be their idea of a perfect world, of a "gay utopia." By definition, utopia is an ideal but imaginary society, a place that doesn't exist. But perhaps some day it will.

"Utopia would be where people are just people and can be themselves, where they can live in an open-minded society, where people are willing to accept everything that is safe and nonviolent."—Brandon, 19

"I would love to see people come together, to think of humor instead of anger."—Joe, 19

"I would inform others that just because we're lesbian or gay doesn't mean we have a disease and we're not contagious."—Aprill, 14

"In a perfect society, the terms *gay, lesbian*, and *bisexual* would have no meaning. Who a person prefers to sleep with would not be integral to determining his or her identity. I believe that the gay, lesbian, and bisexual community came about as a reaction to general societal intolerance. In a truly tolerant world, people wouldn't think so much in terms of 'what' you are but 'who' you are."
—Shawn, 20

"If parents, friends, school, and communities were

completely supportive and accepting, I would have a perfect utopian lifestyle. If I were able to show my emotions and pride at school and the people would react positively, I would be more than happy."—Jolene, 16

"Churches of all denominations need to preach love and acceptance instead of hate and indifference. Everyone needs to realize we are all human and therefore should be treated with equal respect."—Chris, 21

"A Utopia for me would be a public school system open to lesbian, gay, and bisexual youth, where today's youth can feel comfortable expressing themselves without fear or persecution. It would be a place where they can freely embrace their true selves and live with the serenity of knowing that they are just as important as everyone else."—Jody, 21

"I'm straight, but if it were up to me, everyone would be loved and accepted for their personality and their love for others. Whether or not they are gay, bisexual, or lesbian, black or white, male or female, wouldn't matter. Love is love, no matter what!"—Becky, 18

"I want my parents to love me. I want my brother to talk to me. I want to walk in the park holding my girlfriend's hand. I want acceptance, not 'tolerance,' taught in all schools. I don't want secret code words, knowing glances, whispered conversations. I don't want to have to 'come out.' I want to already be there. I want the next march I go to to be so inclusive, so open and free, that it just turns out to be a celebration, with no one left to watch, jeer, or taunt. I want who I love to be secondary to that I love."—Jean, 21

"Utopia? For people to stop asking, 'what made you this way?'"—Tabatha, 19

"A world without AIDS."—Eveco, 22

"Acceptance and understanding from people in general would make life much better for gay, lesbian, bisexual, and transgendered youth. With acceptance and understanding would come the removal of hatred and fear that many people have toward lifestyles that they don't consider 'normal.' Coming out would not be a painful, alienating experience, it would just happen naturally, as the knowledge of their sexual orientation happens for 'straight' youth."—Anthony, 19

"I look forward to the day when my lover and I can walk down the street hand in hand and not have to worry about anything."—Frank, 18

"Love, life, freedom, and peace to all."—Eric, 22

RESOURCES

*"You can get real support through a center. . . .
Just hang in there because we are out there."*
—*Stefani, age 20*

*"My [youth program] has empowered me simply
because it has been there for me, enabling me to
meet other gay youth, get involved with different
activities, and educate myself about safer sex."*
—*Joe, age 19*

There are thousands of community centers and social
service organizations around the country—far too many
to list here—that can give you help and support. We have
listed below, by state and city, the larger community centers and youth programs in the United States. By calling
the center nearest you, you can find out about their youth

programs and get referrals to any other youth groups and organizations which may be closer to you, as well as find out about lesbian, gay, and bisexual youth social events, religious groups, sports teams, and so on. If you need medical or legal help, these groups can also put you in touch with a doctor or lawyer in your area. Some centers also have a pen pal program or a call-in line you can phone to talk to other gay youth.

In addition to general services for gay youth, a growing number of lesbian, gay, and bisexual community centers have begun Anti-Violence Projects. These programs gather information and statistics on hate crimes and domestic violence and offer services and referrals to victims of these types of crimes. The symbol ⊗ indicates the community centers that offer these services. You can call or write to the Anti-Violence Project, 647 Hudson Street, New York, NY 10014, (212) 807-6761, to get the name and address of the anti-violence program nearest you.

There are two organizations that have complete listings of lesbian, gay, and bisexual youth centers, which they update regularly. The Hetrick-Martin Institute publishes the *You Are Not Alone Directory* for a suggested donation of $5.00. You can order the directory or find out about the Institute's many youth programs by phoning (212) 674-2400. The Bridges Project of the American Friends Service Committee at (215) 241-7133 can also refer you to youth groups in your area.

COMMUNITY CENTERS
AND SOCIAL SERVICES

 Anti-violence project

 Pen pal program

 Chatline

ARIZONA

 Phoenix: Valley of the Sun Gay and Lesbian Community Center
602-265-7283

Tucson: Wingspan Youth Group
602-624-1779

ARKANSAS

Little Rock: Women's Project
501-372-0009

CALIFORNIA

Culver City: Lambda Youth Network
Pen Pal Program
 PO Box 7911
Culver City, CA 90233
310-216-1316

Garden Grove: Young Adult Program–Gay and Lesbian Center of
   California
714-534-0862

Los Angeles: Gay and Lesbian Community Services Center
Youth Outreach Pen Pal Program
1625 N. Schrader Blvd.
Los Angeles, CA 90028
213-993-7400

Los Angeles: Gay and Lesbian Youth Talkline
213-462-8130 or 818-508-1802

Sacramento: Lambda Community Center
916-442-0185

San Diego: Gay Youth Alliance San Diego
619-233-9309

117

San Francisco: Bay Area Sexual Minority Youth Network
Pen Pal Program
PO Box 460268
San Francisco, CA 94146-0268
415-541-5012

San Francisco: Lavender Youth Recreation and Information Center
   (LYRIC)
415-703-6150

Santa Barbara: Gay and Lesbian Resource Center Youth Project
805-963-3636

Santa Cruz: Lesbian, Gay and Bisexual Community Center
408-425-LGBC (425-5422)

Santa Rosa: Positive Images
707-433-5333

West Hollywood: Gay and Lesbian Adolescent Social Services (GLASS)
310-358-8727

COLORADO

Colorado Springs: Inside/Out—McMaster Center
719-578-3160

Denver: Gay, Lesbian and Bisexual Community Services Center of
   Colorado—Youth Services
303-831-6268

Fort Collins: Lambda Community Center
970-221-3247

CONNECTICUT

East Norwalk: Tri-Angle Community Center/Outspoken
203-853-0600

Stamford: Gay and Lesbian Guide Line
203-327-0767

DISTRICT OF COLUMBIA

Washington, D.C.: Sexual Minority Youth Assistance League (SMYAL)
202-546-5940

FLORIDA

Gainesville: Gainesville Gay Switchboard
904-332-0700

Miami: Lesbian Gay and Bisexual Community Center, Inc.
305-531-3666

Orlando: Gay and Lesbian Community Services of Central Florida
407-425-4527

Pinellas Park: True Expressions
813-586-4297

St. Petersburg: Family Resources, Inc./Youth and Family Connection
813-893-1150
Sarasota:
813-378-3536

GEORGIA

Atlanta: The Atlanta Gay Center
404-876-5372

Atlanta: Young Adult Support Group
404-876-5372

ILLINOIS

Chicago: Horizons Community Services, Inc.
312-929-HELP (929-4357)

INDIANA

Indianapolis: Indianapolis Youth Group
Pen Pal Program
 PO Box 20716
Indianapolis, IN 46220
317-541-8726

IOWA

Des Moines: Gay and Lesbian Resource Center
515-281-0634

KANSAS

Wichita: The Center
316-262-3991

LOUISIANA

New Orleans: The Lesbian and Gay Community Center of New Orleans
504-522-1103

MAINE

Portland: Outright
207-774-HELP (774-4357)

MARYLAND

Baltimore: Gay and Lesbian Community Center of Baltimore
410-837-5445

Langley Park: BiNet USA
PO Box 7327
Langley Park, MD 20787
202-986-7186
RAIN@GLIB.ORG

MASSACHUSETTS

Boston: Boston Alliance of Gay and Lesbian Youth (BAGLY)
800-42-BAGLY (422-2459)

Boston: Healthy Boston Coalition for Lesbian, Gay, Bisexual and
   Transgendered Youth
617-742-8555

Worcester: Supporters of Worcester Area Gay and Lesbian Youth
   (SWAGLY)
508-755-0005

MICHIGAN

Ann Arbor: Ozone House Gay and Lesbian Youth Group
313-662-2222

Ferndale: Affirmations Lesbian and Gay Community Center
810-398-7105

Grand Rapids: Windfire
616-459-5900

Lansing: Lansing Gay and Lesbian Hotline
517-332-3200

Traverse: Windfire
616-922-4800

MINNESOTA

 Minneapolis: Gay and Lesbian Community Action Council
612-822-0127

Richfield: Storefront/Youth Action
612-861-1675

MISSOURI

St. Louis: Metropolitan St. Louis Lesbian, Gay, Bisexual and Transgendered Community Center
314-997-9897

NEBRASKA

Lincoln: Gay and Lesbian Youth Talkline
402-473-7932

NEW JERSEY

Asbury Park: Gay and Lesbian Community Center of New Jersey, Inc.
908-774-1809

Convent Station: Gay and Lesbian Youth in New Jersey
201-285-1595

New Brunswick: Pride Center of New Jersey
908-846-2232

NEW MEXICO

Albuquerque: Common Bond
505-266-8041

NEW YORK

Albany: Gay and Lesbian Young Adults Support Group (GLYA)
518-462-6138

Bayshore: Long Island Gay and Lesbian Center
516-665-2300

Buffalo: Gay and Lesbian Youth of Buffalo (GLYB)
716-855-0221

New York: Bisexual, Gay and Lesbian Youth of New York (BI-GLYNY)
212-777-1800

New York: Lesbian and Gay Community Services Center
212-620-7310

Rochester: Lighthouse
716-251-9604

Syracuse: Lesbian and Gay Youth Program of Central New York
315-422-9741

Troy: Unity House of Troy, Inc.
518-274-2607

NORTH CAROLINA

Charlotte: Time Out Youth
704-537-5050

Durham: Outright-Triangle Gay, Lesbian and Bisexual Youth
919-286-2396

OHIO

 Cleveland: Lesbian and Gay Community Service Center
216-522-0813

Dayton: YouthQuest
513-274-1616

OKLAHOMA

Oklahoma City: The Oasis Gay, Lesbian and Bisexual Community
Resources Center
405-525-2437

Tulsa: National Resource Center for Youth Services
918-585-2986

OREGON

 Portland: Lesbian Community Project
503-223-0071

Portland: Phoenix Rising
503-223-8299

PENNSYLVANIA

Lancaster: Gay and Lesbian Youth Alliance
717-397-0691

 Philadelphia: The Bridges Project—American Friends Service Committee
215-241-7000

Philadelphia: Penguin Place: Gay and Lesbian Community Center of
Philadelphia, Inc.
215-732-2220

Pittsburgh: Gay and Lesbian Community Center
412-422-0114

PUERTO RICO

San Juan: Fundacion SIDA de Puerto Rico
809-782-9600

SOUTH CAROLINA

Columbia: South Carolina Gay and Lesbian Community Center
803-771-7713

TENNESSEE

Nashville: Center for Lesbian and Gay Concerns
615-297-0008

TEXAS

Austin: Out Youth Austin
512-326-1234

Dallas: Gay and Lesbian Community Center
214-528-9254

 El Paso: Lambda Services
915-562-4297

Houston: Houston Area Teen Coalition for Homosexuals (HATCH)
713-529-3211

VERMONT

Burlington: Outright Vermont
802-865-9677

VIRGINIA

Arlington: Whitman-Walker Clinic
703-358-9550

Richmond: Richmond Organization for Sexual Minority Youth
(ROSMY)
804-353-2077

WASHINGTON

Bellevue: Youth Eastside Services—Bisexual, Gay and Lesbian
Adolescent Drop-In Group (B-GLAD)
206-747-4937

Olympia: Stonewall Youth
206-705-2738

Seattle: Gay, Lesbian and Bisexual Youth Program and Infoline—AFSC
206-632-0500

Tacoma: Oasis Gay, Lesbian and Bisexual Youth Association
206-596-2860

WEST VIRGINIA

Charleston: New Horizons
304-340-3690

WISCONSIN

Madison: "Teens Like Us"—Prevention and Intervention Center for
Alcohol and Other Drug Abuse/Briar Patch
608-246-7606 ext. 142

Milwaukee: Gay Youth Milwaukee
414-265-8500

UNITED KINGDOM HELPLINES

The following organizations provide advice and counseling and can put you in touch with lesbian, gay, and bisexual youth groups and drop-in and community centers in your area.

Aberdeen Lesbian, Gay and Bisexual Switchboard
01224-586-869

The Albert Kennedy Trust
0161-953-4059
Helps young and homeless lesbians, gays, and bisexuals find free lodging throughout England.

Brighton Lesbian and Gay Switchboard
01273-690-825 (Monday to Saturday from 6 P.M. to 10 P.M.; Sunday from 8 P.M. to 10 P.M.)

Cara Friend Belfast
01232-322-023 (Monday, Tuesday, and Wednesday from 7:30 P.M. to 10:00 P.M.)

Edinburgh Gay Switchboard
0131-536-4049 (Every day from 7:30 P.M. to 10:00 P.M.)

Friend West Midlands
0121-622-7351 (Every day from 7:30 A.M. to 9:30 P.M.)
Ring for details about their drop-in center at 37 Thorpe Street, Birmingham B5.

Gay and Lesbian Counselling Southwest
0121-622-7351 (Every day from 7:30 P.M. to 9:30 P.M.)

London Lesbian and Gay Switchboard
0171-837-7324

Manchester Lesbian and Gay Switchboard
0161-274-3999

The National Society for the Prevention of Cruelty to Children (NSPCC)
0800-800-500 (toll-free)
An excellent helpline for any young person who is the victim of physical or sexual abuse.

The Terence Higgins Trust
0171-242-1010 (Every day from noon to 10 P.M.)
Trained counselors answer questions about HIV and AIDS and provide information on available services.

CRISIS HOTLINES

The numbers listed below are all 800 numbers, which means that they are toll free. You will not be charged for your call and the number will *not* appear on your family's phone bill. Except where noted, these hotlines operate 24 hours a day, 7 days a week.

Gay and Lesbian Youth Hotline

800-347-8336 (Monday to Thursday 7 P.M. to 10 P.M.; Friday to Sunday 7 P.M. to 12 A.M.)
Run by the Indianapolis Youth Group, this hotline provides crisis counseling and can refer you to groups in your area that can help you with specific problems.

National AIDS Hotline

800-342-AIDS (342-1437)
800-344-SIDA (344-7431) (Spanish language; every day 8 A.M. to 2 A.M.)
800-243-7889 (for the hearing impaired; Monday to Friday 10 A.M. to 10 P.M.)
Operated by the Centers for Disease Control based in Atlanta, Georgia, this line can provide you with the most up-to-date information on AIDS and HIV. Counselors can also refer you to organizations in your area.

National Runaway Switchboard

800-621-4000
800-621-0394 (for the hearing impaired)
Provides crisis intervention, family mediation, and suicide counseling across the United States; also provides information and referrals for housing, medical services, and counseling; will deliver messages between families and runaways.

Youth Development International

800-HIT-HOME (448-4663)
Provides counseling and referrals to teenagers of all sexual orientations on all youth issues, including substance abuse, physical abuse, homelessness, and health.

Covenant House ("the nine line")

800-999-9999
Covenant House, which has centers in many major cities, including New York, Houston, and New Orleans, provides disenfranchised youth with social services—including housing—and referrals.

Teens Teaching AIDS Prevention (Teens TAP)

800-234-TEEN (234-8336) (Monday to Friday 4 P.M. to 8 P.M.)
Teenagers trained in AIDS prevention answer questions about AIDS and HIV.

RELIGIOUS ORGANIZATIONS

The groups listed below can refer you to a caring religious community or counselor in your area. Many also publish their own newsletters and magazines, which can be subscribed to for a nominal fee.

Baptist

American Baptists Concerned
Oakland, CA
510-530-6562

Brethren-Mennonite

Brethren-Mennonites Council for Gay and Lesbian Concerns
Washington, DC
202-462-2595

Buddhist

Buddhist Association of the Gay and Lesbian Community
PO Box 1974
Bloomfield, NJ 07003

Christian Science

United Lesbian and Gay Christian Scientists
Beverly Hills, CA
818-769-5566

Episcopalian

Integrity, Inc.
Washington, DC
718-720-3054

Evangelical Christian

Evangelicals Concerned
New York, NY
212-517-3171

Judaism

Jewish Information and Support—Rabbi Gottlieb
Albuquerque, NM
505-343-8227

World Congress of Lesbian and Gay Jewish Organizations
PO Box 18961
Washington, DC 20036

Lutheran

Lutherans Concerned
PO Box 10461, Fort Dearborn Station
Chicago, IL 60610

Methodist

Affirmation/United Methodists for Lesbian, Gay and Bisexual Concerns
Evanston, IL
708-733-9590

Metropolitan Community Church (Christians)

Universal Fellowship of Metropolitan Community Churches (MCC)
Los Angeles, CA
213-464-5100

Mormon

Affirmation/Gay and Lesbian Mormons
Los Angeles, CA
213-255-7251

Presbyterian

Presbyterians for Lesbian and Gay Concerns
New Brunswick, NJ
908-932-7501

Quaker

Friends for Lesbian and Gay Concerns
Sumneytown, PA
215-234-8424

Reformed Church Christian

Reformed Church in America Gay Caucus
PO Box 8174
Philadelphia, PA 19101

Roman Catholic

Dignity, Inc.
Washington, DC
800-877-8797

Seventh-Day Adventists

Seventh-Day Adventists Kinship International
Los Angeles, CA
213-876-2076

Unitarian

Unitarian Universalists for Lesbian and Gay Concerns
Boston, MA
617-742-2100

United Church of Christ

United Church Coalition for Lesbian and Gay Concerns
Athens, OH
614-593-7301

NATIONAL AND INTERNATIONAL ORGANIZATIONS

The National Center for Lesbian Rights—Youth Project

San Francisco, CA, 415-392-6257
Lesbian, feminist, multicultural resource center. Services specific to the Youth Project include advice and counseling about legal rights, assistance in accessing youth shelters and social services, referrals to attorneys and patients' rights advocates, referrals to lesbian, gay, bisexual and transgender youth groups and youth advocates, direct legal representation where possible. Other available resources include workshops, videos, and publications.

Gay and Lesbian Parents Coalition International

Washington, DC, 202-583-8029
A worldwide service organization (104 chapters in 8 countries) for lesbian and gay parents, their families, and prospective parents. Services include quarterly newsletters, annual conference, college scholarship fund, media work, and services for youth through COLAGE (Children of Lesbians and Gays Everywhere)

Human Rights Campaign Fund (HRCF)

Washington, DC, 202-628-4160
The nation's largest lesbian and gay political organization. National staff, volunteers, and members throughout the country lobby the federal government on gay, lesbian, and AIDS issues, educate the general public, participate in election campaigns, organize volunteers, and provide expertise and training at state and local levels.

The International Lesbian and Gay Youth Organization (IGLYO: America)

Washington, DC, 202-362-9624
Member organization associations are located throughout Europe. Annual conferences held the first week in August in different European cities give teens and young adults the opportunity to meet other gay youths from around the world. Sponsors a pen-pal program.

National Latino/a Lesbian and Gay Organization (LLEGO)

Washington, DC, 202-544-0092
The only national Latino/a lesbian and gay organization in the U. S. and Puerto Rico, LLEGO provides a resource network of affiliated organizations for Latino/a gays and lesbians, programs designated to funding HIV/AIDS prevention and education projects, annual conferences, lobbying the federal government on issues of particular concerns to the Latino/a community, and two monthly bilingual newsletters.

National Advocacy Coalition on Youth and Sexual Orientation (NACYSO)

Washington, DC, 202-783-4165 ext. 49
Youth members share in all aspects of the organization by running committees, participating in political lobbying, and coordinating campaigns with other non-gay mainstream agencies working to educate the community and improve the lives of lesbians, gays, bisexuals, and non-gay people everywhere.

National Gay and Lesbian Task Force (NGLTF)

Washington, DC, 202-332-6483
A long-standing leader in lobbying and working for gay rights: staff and board positions are held by young members in different divisions of the NGLTF to specifically oversee youth issues.

National Lesbian and Gay Health Association

Washington, DC, 202-939-7880
National coalition composed of lesbian and gay community health centers, care providers, and educators. Programs include education and advocacy at the federal level, a national research institute, technical education and assistance for lesbian and gay health care providers, an annual lesbian and gay health conference, annual publication of the White Paper on the state of lesbian and gay health, as well as extensive HIV-related programs.

Parents, Families and Friends of Lesbians and Gays (PFLAG)

Washington, DC, 202-995-8585
Founded in 1981, this grassroots support, education, and advocacy organization represents more than 27,000 families. Members promote legislation and public policies through local, regional, national, and international coalitions and conferences, and discussion groups. Quarterly newsletters, publications, fact sheets, reading lists, audiotapes, conferences, and seminars are available.

Lambda Legal Defense and Education Fund, Inc.

National Headquarters
New York, NY, 212-995-8585
Works nationally through test-case litigation and public education to defend and extend the civil rights of lesbians, gay men, and people with HIV/AIDS. Founded in 1973, it is the nation's oldest and largest lesbian and gay legal organization. Lambda is *not* a private legal firm so it does not handle routine legal matters, provide legal advice to callers, or recommend attorneys.

SUGGESTED FURTHER
READING

AUTOBIOGRAPHIES AND BIOGRAPHIES

Fricke, Aaron. *Reflections of a Rock Lobster: A Story of Growing Up Gay.* Boston: Alyson Publications, 1995.

Fricke writes about growing up gay in contemporary America, and of the personal, social, and legal battles he fought for the right to attend the prom with the date of his choice, a battle which received national attention. He continues his story in *Sudden Strangers: The Story of a Gay Son and His Father* (New York: St. Martin's Press, 1991), coauthored by his father, Walter.

Johnson, Anthony Godby. *A Rock and a Hard Place: One Boy's Triumphant Story.* New York: Crown, 1993.

The extraordinary autobiography of a fourteen-year-old survivor of child abuse, homelessness, and AIDS. A tough story of real courage told without sentiment.

Navratilova, Martina, with George Vecsey. *Martina.* New York: Fawcett, 1986.

A candid account of one of tennis's most esteemed celebrities, from her sometimes difficult relationship with her parents, to her rise as one of the biggest stars in tennis history, to her much-talked-about love affairs with women and her public affirmation of being a lesbian.

Lives of Notable Gay Men and Women series. Various editors. New York: Chelsea House.

An illuminating series celebrating the lives of gay men and woman who have left their mark on society. Profiles include Liberace, Marlene Dietrich, James Baldwin, Martina Navratilova, Oscar Wilde, Willa Cather, and others.

NONFICTION

Atanasoff, Stevan. *How to Survive as a Teen: When No One Understands.* Scottsdale, Pa.: Harald Press, 1989.

Written by a pastor, this is a down-to-earth guide offering sensible advice on self-esteem, friendships and relationships, sex, romance, and peer pressure.

Balka, Christie, and Andy Rose. *Twice Blessed: On Being Lesbian, Gay and Jewish.* Boston: Beacon Press, 1991.

A landmark anthology of essays by and about lesbians and gays who are seeking ways to celebrate gay pride while actively participating in Judaism.

Borhek, Mary. *Coming Out to Parents: A Two-Way Survival Guide for Lesbians and Gay Men and Their Families.* Cleveland: Pilgrim Press, 1983.

Borhek, who wrote of her own son's coming out in *My Son Eric* (Cleveland: Pilgrim Press, 1979), draws on her experience to help gay men and lesbians and their parents cope with the coming-out process.

The Boston Women's Health Collective. *The New Our Bodies, Ourselves: A Book by and for Women.* New York: Simon and Schuster, 1992.

This outstanding resource contains accessible information on all major women's health issues including HIV/AIDS, violence against women, and environmental and occupational health concerns.

Hunter, Nan D. *The Rights of Lesbians and Gay Men: The Basic ACLU Guide to a Gay Person's Rights.* Carbondale, Ill.: Southern Illinois University Press, 1992.

Using an easy to follow question-and-answer format, the book sets forth the rights of lesbians and gay men under present law and offers suggestions on how these rights can be protected.

Jennings, Kevin. *Becoming Visible: A Reading in Gay and Lesbian History for High School and College Students*. Boston: Alyson Publications, 1994.

An informative, and very readable source encompassing two thousand years of gay history, and focusing on a variety of cultures. A great, accessible reference.

Rafkin, Louise. *Different Daughters: A Book by Mothers of Lesbians*. Pittsburgh: Cleis Press, 1987.

Twenty-five mothers speak candidly about their relationships with their lesbian daughters. Their stories offer comfort and good counsel and add up to a compelling appeal for reconciliation.

Sherrill, Jan-Mitchell. *The Gay, Lesbian and Bisexual Student's Guide to Colleges, Universities and Graduate Schools*. New York: New York University Press, 1994.

Includes the responses of more than 175 schools to a nationwide survey about school policies on gay/lesbian/bisexual issues, including awareness of the extent of homophobia and harassment on the campus, student recommendations about attending the school, and information on housing, accessibility to counseling, and campus organizations.

Singer, Bennett L. *Growing Up Gay/Growing Up Lesbian: A Literary Anthology*. New York: New Press, 1993.

An empowering, eclectic anthology of stories, poems, and essays, featuring works by James Baldwin, Rita Mae Brown, Jeanette Winterson, Dennis Cooper, and Pat Parker among others.

FICTION

Bauer, Marion. *Am I Blue? Coming Out from the Silence*. New York: HarperTrophy, 1995.

A critically acclaimed collection of sixteen short stories about growing up gay by noted writers of young adult literature, including Bruce Coville, Jim Giblin, Francesca Lia Block, William Sleater, Lois Lowry, and others.

Brown, Rita Mae. *Rubyfruit Jungle*. New York: Bantam, 1983.

A classic in gay literature, this is the funny, irreverent story about a lesbian named Molly Bolt. Growing up wretchedly poor in the south doesn't keep her from being smart, sassy, and very proud of her sexual orientation.

Chambers, Aidan. *Dance on My Grave*. New York: HarperTrophy, 1995.

An insightful, elegantly written story about sixteen-year-old Hal's first love experience, a passionate, soulful affair with another young man.

Donovan, John. *I'll Get There. It Better Be Worth the Trip*. New York: HarperCollins, 1989.

Two thirteen-year-old boys who feel like outsiders in their own families turn to each other for friendship and support and develop a deeply affectionate relationship.

Donovan, Stacey. *Dive*. New York: Dutton, 1994.

Fifteen-year-old Virginia is having difficulty coping with her father's illness and her best friend's desertion. The one thing not causing a conflict is her relationship with Jane, which is presented as perfectly natural and very romantic.

Fox, John. *The Boys on the Rock*. New York: St. Martin's Press, 1994.

A popular student and athlete at a strict Catholic school falls in love with a twenty-year-old young man who is also an aspiring politician.

Futcher, Jane. *Crush*. Boston: Alyson Publications, 1995.

When Jinx develops a crush on beautiful, popular Lexie, a student at her private girls' school, she does everything to make it go away. A story rich in romance, attraction, and awakening sexuality.

Garden, Nancy. *Annie on My Mind*. New York: Farrar, Straus and Giroux, 1992.

The tender, bittersweet story of Liza, an intelligent, successful senior in a wealthy New York City school, and Annie, a senior at a middle-class public school. Their friendship blossoms into a love affair that is put to the test.

Homes, A. M. *Jack*. New York: Vintage Contemporaries, 1990.

After his parents divorce, fifteen-year-old Jack's peace of mind is shattered when his dad reveals that he's in love with another man. How Jack learns to accept both his father and himself makes for an endearing story.

Kerr, M. E. *Deliver Us From Evie*. New York: HarperTrophy, 1994.

A subtle and thought-provoking story of the lesbian daughter of a rural Missouri family, narrated by her eighteen-year-old brother Parr. Self-interests drive the family to try to break up Evie's love affair with Patsy, but all their attempts backfire.

Meeker, Richard. *Better Angel*. Boston: Alyson Publications, 1987.

Kurt knows he's different from the other boys, and "different" is a hard thing to be in a small town where everybody knows you—or do they? A winning tale, first published in 1933, about a young man's search for love, companionship, and himself.

Miller, Isabel. *Patience and Sarah*. New York: Fawcett, 1994.

In puritanical nineteenth-century New England, two young women do the unspeakable—they fall in love. Based on the lives of painter Mary Ann Willson and her companion, this inspirational story celebrates women's quest for personal freedom.

Mullins, Hilary. *The Cat Came Back*. Tallahassee: Naiad, 1993.

Seventeen-year-old Stephanie (Stevie) writies of her last six months at an exclusive Connecticut prep school; months filled with confusion, sexual awakening, and self-acceptance. Stevie extricates herself from an abusive relationship with a male teacher and struggles to come to terms with her intense feelings for Andrea, a fellow classmate.

Renault, Mary. *The Persian Boy*. New York: Vintage Contemporaries, 1988.

A fictionalized biography of Alexander the Great, the gay Macedonian king who conquered Greece, Egypt, and the Persian Empire, all before his death at age 33. A beautifully written, engaging read.

Salat, Cristina. *Living in Secret*. New York: Dell, 1994.

When her parents divorce, Amelia wants to live with her mother, but her fathers says no because her mother is a lesbian. So Amelia and her mom run away, erasing all traces of the past as they go. But living in secret can't last forever.

Scoppettone, Sandra. *Happy Endings Are All Alike*. Boston: Alyson Publications, 1991.

High school seniors Peggy and Janet are in love—and trapped in a small town with parents and friends they must learn to confront. Sensitive and well-told.

Scoppettone, Sandra. *Trying Hard to Hear You*. Boston: Alyson Publications, 1991.

Camilla and her best friend Jeff are members of a teen theater group. But when Jeff is discovered kissing the production assistant, Phil, the group angrily turn their backs on Jeff and Phil. Will Camilla and the others learn to understand and accept them?

138

Shannon, George. *Unlived Affections*. Boston: HarperCollins, 1989.

Willie's grandmother never gave him satisfactory answers to the questions he asked about his parents. But after she dies, Willie discovers letters exchanged by his parents that begin to reveal the past—including his father's realization of his homosexuality.

Snyder, Anne. *The Truth About Alek*. New York: NAL Dutton, 1987.

The star quarterback of the high school football team is straight. His best friend is gay. And their friendship is unshakable—until the rumors begin.

Walker, Alice. *The Color Purple*. New York: Pocket, 1989.

The eloquent, memorable, Pulitzer Prize–winning story of a woman named Celie, and the sympathetic relationships she develops with other black women searching for themselves—including the beautiful blues singer who was her abusive husband's lover, but ultimately becomes hers.

Walker, Kate. *Peter*. New York: Houghton Mifflin, 1993.

Fifteen-year-old Peter proves himself to a macho Australian dirt-bike gang, while he quietly dreams of becoming a photographer. Peter feels an attraction to his older brother's gay friend David, and when he's caught hugging David, he begins to think he must be gay, too.

Woodson, Jacqueline. *From the Notebooks of Melanin Sun*. New York: Scholastic, 1995.

When Melanin's single mom announces that she is in love with a white woman, thirteen-year-old Melanin begins to question his own sexuality even as he struggles to find the understanding "light" within himself.

BIBLIOGRAPHY

Suggested further reading is indicated by an asterisk*.

Quotations otherwise uncredited are from author interviews with the Reverend Elder Dr. Charley Arehart, Rabbi Susan Freeman, and lesbian, gay, and bisexual youth, or from responses to a questionnaire distributed nationwide to gay and lesbian centers by the authors.

Alexander, the Reverend Scott W., ed. *The Welcoming Congregation: Resources for Affirming Gay, Lesbian and Bisexual Unitarian Universalists*. Boston: Beacon Press, 1992.

The Alyson Almanac: 1994–1995 Edition. Boston: Alyson Publications, 1993.

Be Yourself: Questions and Answers for Gay, Lesbian and Bisexual Youth. Washington, D.C.: The Federation of Parents and Friends of Lesbians and Gays [PFLAG], 1994.

Bell, Don, comp. *Religion and Spirituality: A Checklist of Resources for Lesbians and Gay Men*. Chicago: American Library Association Gay and Lesbian Task Force, 1994.

140

Boswell, John. *Christianity, Social Tolerance and Homosexuality.* Chicago: University of Chicago Press, 1980.

*Clark, Don. *Loving Somone Gay.* New York: Dutton, 1978; Berkeley: Celestial Arts, 1987.

Cohen, Susan and Daniel. *Teenage Stress.* New York: Dell Publishing, 1992.

*Cohen, Susan and Daniel. *When Someone You Know Is Gay.* New York: Dell Publishing, 1989; New York: M. Evans and Co., 1992.

Cowan, Thomas. *Gay Men and Women Who Enriched the World.* Boston: Alyson Publications, 1988, reprint 1992.

Duberman, Martin, Martha Vicinus, and George Chauncey, Jr. *Hidden from History: Reclaiming the Gay and Lesbian Past.* New York: Meridian, 1990.

Faderman, Lillian. *Odd Girls and Twilight Lovers: A History of Lesbian Life in Twentieth-Century America.* New York: Plume, 1992.

*Fairchild, Betty, and Nancy Hayward. *Now That You Know: What Every Parent Should Know About Homosexuality.* San Diego: Harcourt Brace and Co., 1989.

Gibson, Paul. "Gay Male and Lesbian Youth Suicide." In *Report of the Secretary's Task Force on Youth Suicide.* Washington, D.C.: U.S. Department of Health and Human Services, 1989.

Gordon, Sol. *When Living Hurts.* New York: Dell, 1988.

Griffin, Carolyn, and Marian and Arthur Wirth. *Beyond Acceptance.* New York: St. Martin's Press, 1990.

Hamer, Dean, and Peter Copeland. *The Science of Desire: The Search for the Gay Gene and the Biology of Behavior.* New York: Simon and Schuster, 1994.

Harbeck, Karen M., ed. *Coming out of the Classroom Closet.* Binghamton, N.Y.: Harrington Park Press, 1992.

Hein, Karen, M.D., and Theresa Foy DiGeronimo. *AIDS: Trading Fears for Facts.* Yonkers, N.Y.: Consumer Reports Books, 1991.

141

Herdt, Gilbert, and Andrew Boxer. *Children of Horizons: How Gay and Lesbian Teens Are Leading a New Way Out of the Closet.* Boston: Beacon Press, 1993.

Herdt, Gilbert, ed. *Gay and Lesbian Youth.* Binghamton, N.Y.: Harrington Park Press, 1989.

Is Homosexuality a Sin? Washington, D.C.: The Federation of Parents and Friends of Lesbians and Gays [P-FLAG], 1992.

Johnson, O. D. *What the Bible Says about Homosexuality.* Kansas City, Mo: Alternate Studies Project, n.d.

LeVay, Simon. *The Sexual Brain.* Cambridge, Mass.: MIT Press, 1994.

Levy, Barrie. *In Love and in Danger: A Teen's Guide to Breaking Free of Abusive Relationships.* Seattle: Seal Press, 1993.

Making Schools Safe for Gay and Lesbian Youth: Breaking the Silence in Schools and in Families. Boston: The Governor's Commission on Gay and Lesbian Youth, 1993.

*Marcus, Eric. *Is It a Choice?: Answers to Three Hundred of the Most Frequently Asked Questions about Gays and Lesbians.* San Francisco: HarperSanFrancisco, 1993.

Marcus, Eric. *Making History: The Struggle for Gay and Lesbian Equal Rights.* New York: HarperCollins, 1993.

McNaught, Brian. *On Being Gay.* New York: St. Martin's Press, 1988.

Miller, Neil. *In Search of Gay America: Women and Men in a Time of Change.* New York: HarperCollins, 1990.

Miller, Neil. *Out in the World: Gay and Lesbian Life from Buenos Aires to Bangkok.* New York: Random House, 1993.

Shilts, Randy. *And the Band Played On: Politics, People, and the AIDS Epidemic.* New York: Viking, 1993.

Whitlock, Katherine. *Bridges of Respect: Creating Support for Lesbian and Gay Youth.* Philadelphia: American Friends Service Committee, 1989.

INDEX